LITTLE STRANGER

LITTLE STRANGER

THE WEB of SILENCE DUET
1

LEIGH RIVERS

Little Stranger: A Dark Taboo Romance

Copyright © 2023 by Leigh Rivers

All rights reserved.

This is a work of fiction. Names, characters, places and incidents are created by the author or used fictitiously. Any resemblance to actual persons, living or dead, events or places is purely coincidental.

Edited by Laura at Ten Thousand Editing and Book Design

Proofread by Kendra Taylor, Shawna Peak and
Lauren at PumpkinSpicedReader

Cover and interior formatting by Justine Bergman at JAB Design Studio

ISBN (Paperback): 978-1-7394330-6-2
First Edition 2023

CONTENT WARNING

Don't be fooled by part one, this book is one of the darkest I've ever written and contains a lot of triggering content that some readers may find unsettling.

If dark and taboo books aren't for you, then this isn't your jam. Really, if anything listed triggers you, I beg you to stop now, think about your mental health, and send this book back to where you found it in the pits of hell.

The characters are foster siblings, **not** blood related, but are raised together.

If you are comfortable with heavy somnophilia, CNC, dubious consent, drugging, branding, choking, sex over a dying body, with other kinks like brother-sister kink, knife play, primal play, blood play, pain, screwdriver, fear, light breeding, anal and spider play, Malachi Vize—my new favorite mute psychopath—is waiting for you.

PLAYLIST

Dark Things – ADONA

Sick Obsession – Landon Tewers

Twisted – MISSIO

One Way Or Another – Until The Ribbon Breaks

Archangel – MEJKO, Rose Ghould

HEARTBEAT – Isabel LaRosa

Scars – Boy Epic

In Flames – Digital Daggers

Vendetta – UNSECRET, Krigarè

Hotel Drive – VICE MONROE

M3rry Go – VICE MONROE

Young And Beautiful – Lana Del Ray

Wildest Dreams – Taylor Swift

Listen now on **Spotify**
Little Stranger — Author Leigh Rivers

 Spotify

If a masked stranger presses a screwdriver to your throat and tells you to run, what do you do?

PART ONE

OLIVIA

CHAPTER 1
OLIVIA
Aged 7

Mommy holds my hand as I bounce on my sparkly pink dolly shoes excitedly. The airport is very noisy from all the people rushing around, crowds running with their suitcases ready to go on the big plane!

"Is he here yet?" I ask with a huge grin, pulling Mommy's hand and bouncing some more.

"Not yet, sweetie," she replies, glancing at my daddy. He doesn't seem as excited as me and Mommy, but I did overhear them talking this morning, and he's looking forward to finally meeting him.

My new brother. He's a year older than me, and from what I heard by listening in to my parents, he's been abused, a word they used when they adopted me too.

Daddy places a hand on top of my head to stop me from jumping up and down. He doesn't like it when I do that. He usually hits my butt then sends me to my room.

"Stop being erratic. Do you promise to be on your best behavior, angel?"

I nod enthusiastically and grin, raising my pinkie. "I promise."

He doesn't hook his pinkie with mine, and I drop my hand and pout.

But then my mommy squeals and leans down to me. "Sweetie, this is your new brother. Remember when me and Daddy rescued you from that evil place? We rescued him too!"

A boy walks towards us with a plastic bag—where is his suitcase? He's taller than me, with black hair and the bluest eyes—like the color of my favorite doll's hair.

The lady holding his hand rolls her eyes and mouths, "Good luck," to Mommy then hands some papers to Daddy. "Sign all of these. The last page is about his therapist—please keep that one and scan it over once you've read it all and agree for him to attend each session."

Daddy huffs. "Are you sure about this? Have you considered his report?"

He's looking at Mommy, who narrows her eyes at him. "Yes, Jamieson. You're the one who showed me his case in the first place, so either put a smile on your face or I'll do this myself."

Daddy smiles.

I flap the tulle of the princess dress I wore to surprise him. I want him to be as happy as I am, but he isn't grinning or clapping like me. He looks… sad. Mommy said I cheer her up when I talk to her, so I step forward.

"Hi!" I say with a huge smile. "My name is Olivia. I'm seven!" I hold up seven fingers. "Do you think I look like a princess?" I gesture to my dress.

The boy stares at me, taking one step closer, making me look up at him. He's like the fireman who took me out the burning house—a big, walking, human tower!

Why isn't he saying hello? Doesn't he like my dress?

Instead of speaking, he tilts his head a little—watching me.

My smile drops. "You don't like my dress?" It has pink sparkles to match the ribbons in my hair. Mommy even let me wear some of her juicy lip gloss to make my lips sparkle like twinkling stars.

He does something with his hands, and I narrow my eyes then look at Mommy. She's talking to the lady, and my daddy is writing on pieces of paper. I turn to the boy, and he does the thing with his hands again.

"Was it scary on the plane? I always cry when it goes really fast and shoots off into the sky! Daddy always makes us go on one. He's your daddy now too!"

He just stares at me, lifting his hand to the back of his neck then messing up his curly black hair.

I go to turn to my parents again and gasp when the boy takes my wrist, making my eyes snap back at him. He's moving his hands again, and I blink at him.

Confused, I tilt my head like he did a minute ago, making my brown hair cover my eyes.

He points to the revolving doors then offers me his hand. Mommy and Daddy are still talking to the lady, so I let him take my hand, and we run towards the door. Maybe he wants to play hide-and-seek? I'm really good at finding great hiding places.

I giggle as my dolly shoes hit the ground, my hair flying around crazy.

When I was at the other house, the girls and boys always played games—the boys would chase us, and if they caught us, we had to go to jail. There were so many of us. I had loads of friends! But then Mommy and Daddy came and found me and brought me to their home.

It's so big, and my mommy said I could get a dog for my birthday if I behave. It will be my first birthday with them, and I can't wait to get my first ever present.

"Where are we going?" I ask when he keeps pulling me through the airport, dodging all the busy people way taller than us. I trip up, and I squeal as I tumble forward, but the boy catches me, dragging me back to my feet.

We run again, and I start to laugh again. The boy stops at a door and looks around us, then pulls me inside. I gasp and try to get back out when I see we're in a bathroom full of boys.

Grabbing me to make me look up at him, he does something

with his hands again then points at himself. When I still have no idea what he's doing, he points to his mouth and shakes his head—then points to my mouth and nods.

"You can't talk?"

He shakes his head again, and my eyes widen. "That's okay. I couldn't talk for so, so long! I can teach you."

Annoyed, he rolls his eyes. That's so rude!

He points at me again then presses his palm to his chest, and there's something scary in his eyes as he comes closer to me; I want to go back to our parents. But before I can ask what he's doing or scream real loud, Daddy throws open the door, and my mommy snatches me up into her arms.

"I told you not to be trouble!" Daddy yells at me.

My eyes shut, and I wait for him to yell some more, but he doesn't.

"And you," he snaps at the boy. "You're on a strike, little man. Two more, and your ass is going to *another* new home. You're Malachi Vize now, and the Vizes don't step out of line, so get used to it."

My lips curl into a smile. I'm a Vize too. We aren't afraid of anything.

Except spiders—they creep me out.

The boy lowers his head and circles his fist against his chest.

"He's saying he's sorry, sweetie," Mommy whispers to me. "He communicates with sign language."

"What's that? I want to do it too!"

She chuckles and kisses my forehead. "I'll teach you. We'll teach the whole house."

"Even the house helpers?"

She nods and tucks a lock of hair behind my ear. "Yes. We'll ensure the chefs, maids, and security guards know how to sign. Malachi will be comfortable in our home. He's one of us now."

My new mommy is nice. She never yells at me or scares me like my daddy. She always braids my hair and paints my nails and sings with me in the car.

I like my mommy.

In the car, Malachi sits next to me and stares at me the whole drive home. It's a little weird, and he's making me a little nervous. I smile at him anyway, but he only slants his head, as if he's studying me. He keeps staring at my hair. Maybe he likes my ribbons?

When we get to my room, the one we now share because our mommy thinks it will be the best way for us to "bond," he sits on his bed opposite mine and watches me show him my new dollhouse. He doesn't laugh when I make a joke, or when I make my Barbie talk to him, and when I give him one of my dolls so he can play with me, he pulls the head off and makes my eyes widen.

"No!" I yell, snatching it from him. "You don't do that, Malachi!"

He points at me again then lays a palm on his chest.

"What does that mean?" I ask, popping the doll's head back on and hiding her in the wooden house. "Can you teach me?"

All he does is smirk, then he reaches for a strand of my hair, rubbing it between his fingers.

"Do you want to smell it? It smells like strawberries!"

He brings my hair to his nose and inhales, closing his eyes. I freeze when he pulls me in for a hug. It's a big hug. He's holding the back of my head to his chest and sniffing my hair. I giggle when he brushes his fingers through it.

He pulls back and does something with his hands again, and I grab some paper and hand him a pack of crayons. "Can you write? If not, I can teach you that too."

I watch him take the black one and write down one word that makes no sense.

Mine.

CHAPTER 2
OLIVIA
Aged 11

"And when you press the keys together, you get this." The piano sounds as my tutor shows me how to play "Happy Birthday." She's been teaching me for the last two weeks, and I asked if she could show me how to do that song, so I can play it for Malachi.

He's twelve today, but he doesn't want a party or to go for a family day out. If anything, he seems sad. My hugs usually make him feel better, or when I lie next to him in bed and we watch movies, but he said no when I asked earlier.

Well, he signed "no" because he still doesn't talk. Mom said it's selective—he chooses not to speak, and hasn't since he was five years old. I'm not sure why; my dad said he'd explain when I'm older.

Sometimes, when we lie in bed or the tent we pitch in the living room, I'll try to coax him or trick him into talking, which only makes him mad—he'll ignore me for days when I do that.

My friends think he's weird for not talking and laugh when he signs to me, but I tell them to shut up.

We still share a room. Mom wanted to move him into his own one, but he begged her to let him stay. He's scared of the dark and sometimes sleeps beside me. And I don't think he likes Dad very much. Malachi ran out of his office with a black eye the other day.

I look up from the piano as Malachi walks in. He's wearing a black hoodie, the hood up, nearly covering his curly black hair. He sits on the sofa in front of the piano and watches me while I finish my lesson.

My tutor goes to speak to Mom, something about having to reschedule my next lesson, and they get into a discussion. I hear them talk about Malachi's birthday, that my dad won't be here since he's intentionally working late.

Malachi comes to sit on the stool beside me. He signs, *Teach me?*

He watches my fingers as I play to him what I just learned, and his eyes light up when he realizes what it is. I grin and shrug. "Happy birthday," I say quietly. "It was supposed to be a surprise."

He signs, *Thank you*, then gestures to the piano again. *Play.*

This time, I mess up, and he silently laughs at me when I huff and cross my arms—then he starts to press the keys in front of him, higher-pitched, and I try not to giggle at his terrible piano skills.

"Did you like the present I got you? Mom helped me pick it."

He nods then kisses my cheek, signing, *Thank you.*

I turn my cheek and point at the other one. He kisses that, then I point at my forehead, and he kisses that too. When I point to my nose, he kisses my lips, and I freeze.

Pulling back, I stare at him, wide-eyed. "Mom told me not to let boys kiss me! You're a boy!"

I'm your brother, so I'm allowed.

"Really?"

He nods, his eyes flashing. He watches me for a long second then turns his body, pressing the piano keys again.

I glance over my shoulder and notice my mom standing in the doorway, looking concerned as she holds Malachi's birthday cake—the candles already melting.

Later that night, Dad comes home and drags Malachi out of bed, and when I try to ask what's wrong, he yells at me to go back to sleep.

When Malachi comes back to our bedroom hours later, he's visibly shaking and apologizes to me using his hands, and I hug him until he falls asleep.

I brush my hair in the mirror, pull it into a high ponytail to keep it out of my face, swipe on some mascara, then hunt for my favorite lip gloss. If I don't hurry, I'm going to be late for cheer practice, and as the captain, I need to be responsible and try to be there at least twenty minutes before everyone else.

My vanity shakes as I slam the little drawer, and I let out a long, annoyed breath. "Where is it?" I mutter, searching through my makeup bags again. I pull my school bag across the floor then scan the rest of my room.

I bend down to look in my school bag again just as a knock sounds on the room door.

Malachi stands in my doorway, holding up my lip gloss.

"Why do you have that?" I ask him, frowning. Then my brows soften. "Did I leave it in the kitchen again?"

He nods and silently steps in, closing the door behind him. He tosses my lip gloss to me then pulls off his cap, turning it backwards to tame his wavy hair.

Over the last year, Malachi has changed from a boy to a young man. For seventeen, he looks twenty with a chiseled jaw, long lashes, and bright, diamond-like blue eyes. He has muscles that are starting to become noticeable through his clothes, and he loves to run. He once signed to me that it helps clear his head.

Sometimes, we run together. We'll listen to the same song— usually Taylor Swift if I choose, or Bad Omens if he does— then we'll sit by the lake and watch the sunrise before we go home and get ready for school.

All my friends want to kiss him. He's the quiet, mysterious Malachi Vize that everyone wants a piece of. It sickens me— especially when they go into detail in the group chat about things I'd rather not read. He's not popular—he's the "silent weirdo," yet they say things behind his back because they're too scared to say anything to his face.

Malachi leans down and sniffs my hair, just like he does every day, then sits on my bed and signs, *Where are you going?*

"Abigail's having a sleepover. Dad said I could go."

His eyes darken a touch, and his jaw tightens.

He does that a lot too.

"Are you going out?" I ask him, and he shakes his head.

By going out, I mean on the motorbike Mom got him for his seventeenth birthday. He drives around like a lunatic, and he thinks our parents don't know he smokes, but we can all smell it coming from his room on the other side of Vize Manor.

Mom moved him into his own room after he kissed me on the lips in front of them. It was innocent. We'd just won a board game together and were celebrating. Apparently the wrong way.

Watching them empty his side of the room was the worst day of my life—and probably his. I've never felt lonely, not since Mom and Dad adopted me; Malachi was always here, keeping me company, especially on stormy nights.

My nightmares have come back, and sometimes, when I can't even breathe because of them, I sneak over to his room. He never turns me away—he misses sharing a room with me too.

We used to push our beds closer and hold hands, and he sometimes sat on the edge of my bed until I fell asleep. He's such a protective brother. Always making sure I'm okay. Even years later, I hate that he's on the other side of the house.

Stay, he signs. *Watch a movie with me.*

"I already said I would go. We can watch a movie tomorrow night," I say, swiping the gloss onto my lips and puckering them in the vanity mirror. I pout at him in my reflection. "Aw, is my big brother going to miss me?"

He gets up from my bed, and I gasp as he grabs my hair and pulls my head back. Taking my cheek with his other hand, he swipes the sticky lip gloss across my mouth with his thumb.

My brother pulls my bottom lip down, watching it snap back. He looks… mesmerized?

And for some reason, I'm stuck in a trance too as he grabs my chin, pulling my hair hard enough that I hiss, yet I don't fight him or tell him to stop. A part of me wants him to tug harder—I want him to… something.

What's happening?

He releases me and backs away, his chest rising and falling as if he's trying to control himself. Malachi stares down at his thumb, shining with gloss from my lips, then at my now messy hair.

My breaths are heavy as I wipe my mouth, my heart racing in my chest, confused about how I feel and why I'm so flushed.

The chair I'm on is rolled back into position in front of my vanity, and Malachi takes my hairbrush, pulling my pony from the hair tie, then starts to drag the brush through my hair as if nothing just happened.

Three days later, Mom is cutting vegetables when I enter the kitchen, the radio playing quietly as she hums along to the song. Dad is at work, as always. If he doesn't have his nose buried in some paperwork, he's on a conference call or at court, representing some crazy person who's trying not to get life imprisonment for murdering six people in one night.

The Vizes are famous for the cases that usually plaster news channels and social-media platforms worldwide. Dad is a criminal defense attorney, and my mom is a judge. However, ever since she adopted me and Malachi, she works less and less and paints in her art room while we're at school.

I don't remember much of my life before being here, but I do remember how my body felt when I went days without food; when my drug addict of a mother let men in and out the house; the way my baby brother stopped crying forever. He lay there in his crib for days before child services burst in and found his decaying body cradled in my arms.

Apologizing over and over again for not saving him, I was rushed to the emergency room, and a week later, the Vizes introduced themselves and said they'd make sure I never knew what it felt like to go hungry again.

They kept their word.

Even though I'm scared of my dad, I love him. He's heavy handed with Malachi and swears like a sailor, but he's trying to be calmer, better. He no longer consumes alcohol and keeps himself busy. I can't say Malachi receives the same treatment from him as I do. The only reason my brother is still under this roof is because Mom and I love him, and he's a part of our family regardless.

Said brother walks into the kitchen behind me, his shoulder brushing mine, then ruffles his hair as he stares into the refrigerator and grabs an orange juice. His eyes slide to Mom then to me, and something shines in his eyes.

I did go to my friend's house the other night, but I snuck out when everyone fell asleep, and instead of climbing in my own window, I climbed right into Malachi's.

But that's a normal thing siblings do, right?

CHAPTER 4
OLIVIA
Aged 18

"I think I hate you."

Malachi looks offended as we walk out of the store he just bought his arachnid from. The box with holes is hugged to his chest while I unlock my car and grimace when he places the cardboard box in the back seat.

It trembles a little, and I shake my head. "There's no *thinking* about it; I do hate you. If you take it back, I won't revoke the big-brother card."

Stop being scared.

"No. Fuck you. Why, out of all the cute little animals in there, did you buy a tarantula? When you told me you wanted to get a pet, I thought you meant a kitten or a damn dog!"

My brother narrows his eyes at me, so I roll mine and turn on the engine, heading for home. Our parents will still be out— they have some sort of meeting about a new foster kid who could potentially be living here soon.

I hope it's not another brother—I adore Malachi, but he's a lot of work sometimes, especially with his possessiveness. It started to show more when I was sixteen and went out for sleepovers, girls' days, or even to the gym. Every time, without fail, he'd blow up my phone with messages, because obviously he can't call, since he still doesn't talk.

Once, when me and Abbi got drunk at her parents' house and I called him, I slurred every word and sent him my location before losing my phone, and he hunted for me on his motorbike for hours.

When he was forced to give up and come home, he found me asleep in his bed. I woke in the morning with my head on his chest—awfully tangled in his limbs—and the little devil on my shoulder told me to stay, but I knew it was wrong, so I snuck out and went to my own room.

Imagine another one of him in the house? I would go insane. I love him, I really do, but I have strange thoughts about him sometimes. When my fingers slip between my thighs or when I'm kissing someone else, it's shameless how many times his face has been at the forefront of my mind when I find my orgasm.

Then I'd have to sit down for breakfast or dinner or supper with him, our parents too, and pretend I didn't just get off to the thought of my brother.

"I need to get gas," I say when I notice my tank is close to empty. I turn into the closest station and glance at the box over my shoulder and wonder if he'll notice if I accidentally leave it on the roof of someone else's car.

Spiders give me chills. Small ones that run across your room floor, dangle from the ceiling, or casually chill on your face while you sleep are bad enough, but the hairy thing in that box isn't just a little spider—it's red and black and hairy and looks like it might eat me.

Rain patters down, making puddles on the ground as I fight with the handle and the gas cap—Malachi ends up twisting it off for me and sits on the hood while I fill up the tank. Arms crossed, he stares at me, and I narrow my eyes. "What?"

You don't have your lip gloss on.

I rub my lips together—they're stained red from the lipstick I bought a few days ago. "I like this one better."

I disagree. You look like a hooker.

I slap his arm, and he silently laughs.

"Mom wants me to find a boyfriend because apparently I need a man to look after me." I roll my eyes. "She said they'll partner me up with that weirdo Parker."

Malachi's eyes darken, his jaw clenching. *You're only eighteen.*

I laugh. "Tell her that!" Twisting on the gas cap, I pat his shoulder. "Count yourself lucky Dad thinks men are power, or you'd be forced into marriage at a young age too."

He snatches my wrist before I can pull away then drops it to sign a reply. *No, you aren't getting married.*

19

I sigh. "I really suggest you don't fight our parents on this. Their tradition is that I've to be pure and innocent until I'm married, and you can do whatever you want. Just enjoy your freedom."

Before he can respond—probably something angry given the look in his eyes—I turn away, blocking his communication, and head inside to pay and grab some snacks.

While I'm waiting in line, a tap on my shoulder has me jumping and turning, and dropping my bags of chips on the ground. We both lower to our knees to pick them up, and my hand lands on theirs. My eyes lift, and I find Adam, who I used to sit beside in calculus, smiling back at me.

I haven't seen him in months. He dropped out of school and vanished, which was a surprise, since he was one of the best jocks, smart, and—dare I say—handsome?

A voice in the back of my head is yelling at me to grab the chips and leave, but we end up talking for nearly ten minutes while the cashier waits, joining in when we comment on how terrible the weather's been for June, before the bell jingles above the door and Malachi storms in.

His eyes are on the guy I've been talking to, and he looks mad.

No. Furious.

"Oh, sorry, I was just talking to—"

He slams Adam's head into the wall with enough force that

I cringe at the cracking sound. Once, twice, three times, and blood splatters as Adam goes limp on the ground. My eyes are wide, no sound coming out of my parted lips as the cashier runs to call the cops.

Malachi's nostrils are flaring, and he turns to me, grabs my jaw, and signs, *No.*

"I didn't do anything," I breathe. "Why... why did you just do that?" My gaze drops to a passed-out Adam, blood oozing from a cut on his head, and I glance up. "Malachi..."

He shakes his head, lowering his raging gaze to Adam rousing and trying to get up from the floor, then snatches my wrist and pulls me out of the gas station.

He tosses me into the car then slams the door, and I'm frozen, barely blinking as he sits behind the wheel. He's signing something to me, but I'm not looking, my heart racing as he breathes out a huff and speeds out of the gas station.

He drives us home, and I sit in silence, occasionally glancing at his right hand, the one he just used to assault Adam. Shaking, he grips the steering wheel, and I gulp at the bulging veins in his arms, feeling a sensation between my legs that definitely shouldn't be there.

I shouldn't be turned on from watching him attack someone. His violence should be punished. I should be yelling at him for doing that; instead, I'm envisioning him holding me down and...

"Why did you do that?" I ask, trying to keep my tone calm and collected.

But I fail. Why does my voice sound all breathy and needy?

Why are my panties soaked?

Sick. Sick, sick, sick. And shameful.

Malachi ignores me and drives faster.

"He was a friend from school. He knocked into me by accident, and we were only talking. He wasn't being a dick or anything."

Shut up, he signs.

I scowl, crossing my arms. "The cops are going to come for you now, and Dad is going to be so mad, and then Mom will get into a fight with him. Just drop me at Abbi's."

No.

"Malachi. Drop me at Abbi's place or I'll scream."

He glances at me, presses down on the accelerator, and signs, *Then scream.*

I shake my head and look out of the window. He doesn't take me to my friend's house; he drives us both home. As soon as he pulls into the garage, I throw open the door and run to my room.

Mom and Dad get home around the same time the cops arrive, informing them that Adam doesn't want to press charges. The entire time Malachi is unfazed, slouched in a chair with parted legs, his eyes glued to a spot on the wall as he blanks everyone out.

He gets a warning—to be on his best behavior and possibly seek some help.

Mom's eyes are wet, and she keeps glancing at Malachi as if he's going to defend his actions, but he flicks his lighter and ignores them.

"What the hell is wrong with you?" Dad yells at him. "You're lucky he doesn't want any more trouble, or you'd make our family look like a goddamn disgrace!"

Mom sits up. "Adam's family did say they'd drop the charges under certain conditions."

"What conditions?" I ask, and she gives me a warm smile.

"One condition. We promise Olivia to Adam."

Malachi's hands fist, and Dad's eyes widen.

"I thought she had an arrangement with Parker?"

Mom shrugs. "It's always good to have more than one option, Jamieson."

"And how many options do you plan on giving our daughter, Jennifer?"

When they use their names in those tones, things usually explode. Swallowing, I drop my gaze to my lap, embarrassment coursing through me as they argue.

There's a kick against my shin, and I lift my watery gaze to see Malachi staring at me. His brows are knitted together, and while our parents argue, he signs, *I will kill anyone who touches you.*

I believe him.

But this is his fault.

The yelling continues, but he doesn't care. He doesn't even flinch when Dad knocks over the table in frustration. Mom starts shouting at him then, and as things escalate into a competition over who can raise their voices the loudest, Malachi gestures to the door, and we both slip out.

"Thanks," I snap, moving away from his hand low on my back, leading me up the grand staircase. "Because of you, Mom is going to force me to date him too. I hope you're proud of yourself, *big brother*." And I turn away from him, storming left to my room.

"Are you awake, sweetheart?"

I pause the TV and sit up. "Yeah. Come in."

My mom opens the door and closes it quietly behind her, her eyes puffy. She and dad really went to war with each other earlier, and it's obvious she's only just stopped crying.

"Are you okay?" I ask. "You were arguing for hours."

"Your father wasn't pleased about my suggestion that you go on a date with that boy, but it was Adam's parents' condition for not having Malachi charged."

I press my lips together. "So to stop him from getting charged, I need to go on a date. That's blackmail, and quite honestly, it sickens me that you even agreed to it."

"If you don't go, Malachi will get into a lot of trouble."

When I blankly stare at her, she adds, "Do you know why your brother did that today?"

Shaking my head, I reply, "No. I was just talking to Adam. He won't tell me why he did it."

She sighs and sits on the edge of my bed, running her hands through her hair—golden blonde and thick and not a hint of grey, despite Dad's hair being whiter than white.

"He won't talk to us. He hasn't for quite a while—even when I cried for him to communicate with me, he stared right through me. But he'll have a conversation with you."

My shoulder raises. "Yeah. We're close like that."

"Forgive me for asking this, but you can tell me the truth, sweetheart. Has he ever… hurt you?"

My eyes widen, and I sit up straighter. "What? No! Why would he?"

"Malachi isn't like us, Olivia. I'm not sure why we thought we could handle someone like him. So troubled and so… I don't know. His controlling and possessive tendencies over you are dangerous. Even when your father kisses your forehead, Malachi glares at him like he wants to slit his throat. He won't speak to a therapist and won't touch medication, and I fear he really needs both."

"Why would he need them?"

She nibbles her lip and flattens her lips. "Malachi has... issues. As well as all the trauma from his life before coming here that triggered his mutism, he isn't mentally normal. Have you ever heard of ASPD?"

"Sure, but Malachi isn't a psychopath or anything. He's just quiet and has a temper."

Mom shakes her head. "He was diagnosed at fifteen, sweetheart. And... your father and I think that, maybe, we should ask him to leave now that he's nineteen and at an age to support himself."

My teeth crush together as I throw my duvet off. "No," I force out. "If he goes, I go."

"Don't be stupid, Olivia. Why would you do that? Malachi needs space and no restrictions, and if he's living under our roof, he needs to abide by our rules. Your father can't even be in the same room with him without feeling uncomfortable. You can't leave—you have... ties to our family. You're a Vize."

"I promise you, Mom, if Malachi goes, I *will* leave with him."

"Very well." Her shoulders hunch, and she gazes at the floor for a long minute. "If he messes up once more, I don't care what the repercussions are. Malachi will be told to leave. We raised him, we put clothes on his back, and filled his stomach with food. We already did our job. He's grown up now and will not bring shame to this family."

"Is that how you feel about me too? You done your job by raising me, so you no longer need to act like a parent? You'll just sell me off to marry someone else's son to secure more money for yourselves?"

"God, no, Olivia. You're my daughter and always will be. I'm not afraid of you, and I don't feel uneasy bringing new fosters in with you here. But Malachi? He seriously assaulted someone just for talking to you. What will happen if a new foster wants to be your friend?"

Burning-hot tears slip down my cheeks. "Malachi is your son."

"He is, and I love him; we all do, but he's dangerous and unhinged and unpredictable. He can't feel remorse or empathy or regret or even love someone properly. He's a weapon."

"Get out," I grit. "Get out and never speak about *your son* like that again."

"I'm just looking out for everyone, sweetheart. If you can speak to Malachi and talk to him about medication and therapy, then we can help him not end up in prison—or, worse, dead from picking a fight with the wrong person. He didn't even consider the cameras or witnesses when he smashed that poor boy's head into the wall."

She tries to place a hand on mine, and I pull away. "I was

speaking to Adam's mother on the phone. He's willing to go for dinner with you this weekend. I can rearrange your date with Parker to the weekend after."

Through my teeth, I grit, "How considerate of him."

"We can go dress shopping tomorrow. Pick you something nice and flattering."

I don't dignify her with a response as she leaves the room, and I hug my knees to my chest, hearing her words over and over again. Part of what she said is right: Malachi is a little… unhinged at times, but he isn't the monster she's trying to paint him as.

Taking out my laptop, I look up "ASPD," checking forums and medical reports, and the more I read, the more I realize that despite everything I feel towards Malachi—caring about him, wanting to spend time with him, and getting butterflies when we sleep in the same bed—he might not feel the same way about me.

But then I inwardly smack myself, because he's my brother, so obviously he's not going to feel the same way I do. He's possessive of me because I'm his sister, not because he wants to fuck me into next week.

How does he see life? If he can't feel certain emotions, then what's it like to live in his shoes? Does he even care about living?

No matter what traits and descriptors say about Malachi's diagnosis, whether he's a psychopath or a sociopath or something else, he's my big brother, and I will *never* walk away from him.

Hours later, when everyone is asleep, I climb out of my window and balance across the ledge to his side of the manor. When I first did this years ago, I was terrified of the drop. Heights and I don't mix, but I've grown used to this one.

He never locks his balcony, so I slide across the door and slip in.

"Archangel" by MEJKO plays from his speaker, low enough that no one else in the house will be able to hear it. The clanking of metal, the gusts of breath he pushes out each time he raises the barbell above his head while laid out on the weight bench, the glistening sweat all over his chest and face—the combination sends a shiver through me, and I stay silent, watching, just like he does when he sees me cheer out in the yard.

He drops the barbell back onto the bench stand and sits up, panting silently and sweating and rubbing the towel across his soaked face. He's only wearing shorts, so his abs are on show, glittering with sweat as he gets to his feet, tossing the towel down and running his fingers through his already disheveled hair.

He looks to the side, his eyes clashing with mine, and I fidget my fingers behind my back. "Hi. I couldn't sleep."

He towers over me, his chest rising and falling as he closes the distance between us, stopping in front of me and reaching for one of my plaits. He slips off the hair tie and unravels my hair, rubbing the strands between his fingers and bringing them to his nose—inhaling and closing his eyes.

Normality for us went out the window a while ago, because I like when he does this. It calms him, and for some reason, it calms me too to know that. I tried to change my strawberry-scented shampoo once, and he threw my new one in the trash and filled my bathroom unit with a supply of the one he loves.

"Why did you do that today?" I whisper, my voice faltering as I look up at him through my lashes. That towering height, mixed with his muscles and dimples... I hate the fact that he's my brother. Why can't he just be a friend's brother, or someone I met by chance?

I'm starting to realize that I might have a crush on Malachi—the world needs to eat me up and spit me into space because *what the hell?*

His silence is deafening, his breaths starting to calm from his vigorous workout.

"Mom told me to speak to you about something."

The tip of his head is slight, and he lets go of my hair and backs away.

"She thinks you need help. A therapist, and to be medicated."

He licks the salty sweat from his lips and reaches for a fresh towel, tossing it over his shoulder. He turns his back to me, and my eyes zone in on the expanse of it. He has a nice back, a tattoo on his ribs travelling up his back and across his shoulders.

It's still fresh—I went with him to get it done a few days ago and read a book for nearly six hours while he kept his eyes on me. I asked if it hurt, but he shook his head.

I would rather stick pins in my eyeballs than get a tattoo. Who wants to be punctured with needles over and over again? No thank you.

He told me that night, while we watched a movie, that he was going to find a tattoo gun and put his name on my thigh, then continued to grab it and make me squeal as he started tickling me. I ended up frustrated and crushing my thighs together while we watched a movie.

Totally normal sibling behavior.

I want that playful Malachi, not the one walking away from me and into his bathroom to turn on the shower. He walks back in, leaning over the glass tank to check on his tarantula.

He looks up. *Come here.*

Hesitantly, I move forward, standing beside him as I watch the eight-legged beast scurry into a burrow. But then Malachi reaches down to grab it, letting it crawl onto his palm, and I try to step back, but he snatches my wrist to keep me in place.

The darkness within his eyes holds me in place, my body trembling as he manipulates my hand to put my palm upwards.

The spider is on the back of his hand as he signs to me. *Are you going out with that dickhead?*

I bite my lip. "I need to. Mom set up a dinner date for the weekend."

His nostrils flare. He signs again. *And the other guy?*

My huff is louder than intended. "You already know I have to. It's what Vize women do apparently. I can't say no."

His jaw ticks, and I yelp as he snatches my wrist.

"Please don't," I beg, barely able to stay still as the spider crawls down his arm, up his forearm, and settles in his palm. "Please, please, please don't."

Malachi tries to put the horrific thing in my palm. I yank away just in time, and it drops onto the floor. The shriek I let out as it scurries to my feet vibrates in my ears as I run to the other side of the room, throwing myself on his bed.

I'm still screaming when Malachi climbs on top of me and covers my mouth with his hand, fingers digging into my cheek. He raises his finger to his lips, telling me to be silent, but all I can focus on is his body layered over mine—the hardness pressed against my inner thigh.

He's... hard. Aroused.

His cock is hard and it's pressing against me.

Me. His sister.

I gulp, tensing everywhere to stop myself from moving, not breathing as I feel him twitch. His jaw is clenched firmer, his eyes hooded as he stares down at me.

I try to say something against his palm, but only a muffled whimper pours out of me.

Is he getting harder?

Oh God.

Not wanting to point out the obvious, because he might not even mean to be hard, or feel the heat between us rising, or the energy in the room altering as my own arousal coats my panties—and because my mouth is covered—I lift my hands to sign.

I won't scream.

He twitches again, and before he gets off me, he pushes down so his cock runs against my clit, and I bite my cheek to suppress a moan.

Sick, I'm so fucking sick. He isn't meaning to do it, but here I am, horny and wanting my brother to press his cock between my legs again. And the way it felt? He's well endowed, that's for sure.

I sit up and go to tell him that I'll sleep in my own room if he wants, but my words are lost when I see the tented, thick outline of his cock through his shorts. He isn't even trying to hide it as his music still plays in the background, his tarantula crawling up his arm to his shoulder.

I lift my eyes to his face, and I think he caught me looking at his dick. He just caught his little sister salivating over his size. Can this night get any worse?

He tilts his head, his hands fisting at his side before he lifts them. *Get into bed. I'll be there in a minute.*

He gestures to my side of the bed and turns away, placing

his spider back in its tank and heading to the shower.

My skin tingles, and the butterflies are going insane, my thighs rubbing together as I lie under the covers and wait. They smell like him, and the way I'm feeling, the scent only makes me worse. I slip my hand between my legs, letting out a soft moan as I finger my wetness. With my eyes glued to the door of the bathroom, where he's naked and wet, I picture him on me again as I sink two fingers inside myself.

The door handle jiggles, and I pull my fingers free, needing to keep going but stopping as he comes out of his bathroom with a new pair of shorts on, rubbing his black wavy hair with a towel before dropping it into his laundry basket.

He climbs into bed beside me, grabs his remote, and turns on the TV. His knee bumps mine, and he doesn't pull it away as his thigh presses to my own, and I wonder if he knows my fingers are still wet, or that my pussy is clenching on nothing, needing something.

Him.

I want to slap myself.

"Promise me you won't beat anyone else up."

No, he signs.

Crossing my arms, I shuffle away from him, but I shriek as he grabs my knee and pulls me back. *Stop being a brat.*

"Every time you attack someone, Mom is probably going to try to arrange a date for me. She's desperate for me to get married young because she did."

His head snaps to me. *How many dates has she arranged?*

"I've been on four so far. Two to go. Yay me."

He straightens. *So far? You've been on dates already?*

Rolling my eyes, I huff. "I'm eighteen."

And? Did you fuck them?

I gasp. "I'm not talking about this stuff with you!"

He tries to sign, but I grab his hand, lacing our fingers. "Watch the movie, Malachi, or I'm going back to my room."

I somehow fall asleep, waking a few hours later to find Malachi plastered to my back. His strong arms encase me as his soft, gentle breaths breeze against my neck, making those forbidden sensations return between my legs.

I can't get back to sleep—especially since his cock is hard as granite and pressing against my ass, his arms tightening around me as I pretend to shift and rub my ass against him.

Then I stop, freezing in place with my eyes wide—did I just… grind my ass against my sleeping brother's dick?

He shifts, and his hand drops to my inner thigh, gripping it, and I stifle a whimper as his fingers dig into my skin.

I want to slide his hand upwards, to press his thick fingers to my clit, to feel his touch—am I insane?

I glance over my shoulder and stiffen when I see that his eyes are open, glaring at me. "Did I wake you?" I ask, trying to ignore his hand; the prodding cock or the fact I just grinded my ass against it.

He shakes his head.

"Are you okay?"

I shouldn't mention the fact he's hard. We've slept in the same bed since we were kids, and I don't think this has ever happened. Sure, he'd have morning wood now and again, and one time I woke up with my hand on his bulge—I never yanked my hand away faster than I did that morning. But right now, we're both awake, and neither of us is moving from our current positions.

I'm still looking over my shoulder, my breath hitching as he tightens his grip on my inner thigh, pulling me firmer against him, causing his cock to press harder between my legs. I part them a little, his head oh so close to my clit. Being so turned on by this is insanity. Maybe I'm the one who needs to see a therapist?

He releases my inner thigh and his fingers twist in my pajama top, causing a button to pop.

He suddenly lets go and rolls onto his back, his arm still under me. He rubs a palm down his face, looking at me again before closing his eyes.

I turn to face him, pressed up to his side, and he doesn't move me away—and when I hike my leg up and onto his thigh, he holds it there.

Wearing sleep shorts was a bad idea—or maybe good, the

skin on skin, and fireworks are going off, my nerve endings sizzling and making me have to fight to keep my breathing steady. He seems to be thinking, brows narrowed, his lips parted as he runs the tip of his tongue along his bottom lip before capturing it with his teeth.

Then Malachi releases my leg and takes my hand, not looking at me as he pulls me even closer, and my eyes widen as he places my hand on his cock over his shorts.

"Malachi…" I hesitate, even as my fingers curl around the thickness of it.

He doesn't respond, or even look at me, but his dick pulses, and when I say his name again, needing him to look at me, to talk to me to confirm what's going on, he gets thicker, harder, thrusting a little into my hand.

I try to pull it away, but his eyes ping open and he stops me.

"I'm your sister," I argue. "We… No, Malachi." Wanting to do something and actually doing it are two different things.

He closes his eyes and raises his hips a little, making our hands rub against himself while he curls my fingers around him again and rocks his hips once more.

"We're brother and sister," I urge, but he's not listening as he drags my hand up to his waistband, pressing it to the taut muscles of his abs, the warmth of his skin, before sliding both of our hands down again.

As much as I want to touch him, to please him, I remind

myself that it's forbidden, and the world would never allow something like this to happen. I'm sick, and if we do this, I'll make him sick too.

I pull away before I reach the heat of his smooth skin.

"We can't," I say firmly. "You know it's wrong."

Don't grind your ass on my cock and I won't accept the invitation.

My mouth falls open, and I'm unable to speak for a long minute, even as he closes his eyes, folds his arm to rest his head on his hand, and shoves his other hand down the front of his shorts, tucking himself into his waistband. I can still see the outline of him, and my mouth waters.

He tilts his head, and I'm caught staring at his cock again.

I flatten my lips and lie back. "Do you see me as your sister?"

Without looking at me, he lifts his free hand and signs one last thing before falling asleep.

You're mine.

CHAPTER 5
OLIVIA

The cuddling in bed alters after that night.

The way he looks at me is still the same, but there's something else there now—something like a deep need or hunger, or maybe it's revulsion at what we nearly did? I'm not sure if he's mad or confused about what happened, or regretful of his actions.

I mean, he did try to put his sister's hand down his shorts. But then again, I did rub myself against him.

I inwardly facepalm when I think of that night two months ago.

We still hang out all the time, and I still refuse to go anywhere near his furry spider, and when we fall asleep either in my bed or his, the cuddles are warmer, our legs are tangled, and I always have a better sleep when I'm with him.

We both know it's frowned upon. Our parents would be mortified if they knew we were this close.

Malachi knows this too. One morning, Mom knocked on my door, and he had to roll off the bed and hide under it while she talked to me again about trying to get him to therapy—as if we were plotting against him. And then thanked me for going on dates with both Adam and Parker, and asked which one I felt more suited to.

I could've smacked her when she said she'd seen me kissing them.

He didn't talk to me for nearly two weeks after that, and it was horrible and lonely and boring.

Then I went to Abbi's for a sleepover and woke in the middle of the night to find Malachi climbing in her window. He shoved his hand over my mouth and made me leave with him. We ended up in my bed, and he fell asleep, but I lay awake for hours, the urge to touch him stronger than ever—hard and pulsing right between my legs while he lightly snored in my ear.

With only myself as a witness, I kissed his cheek while he slept, laced our fingers together, and—when I let curiosity win out—gently let my hand slide from his chest, down his defined abs, so I could dip my fingers under his waistband.

I didn't touch him—not really. I grazed my fingers over the soft skin, felt him twitch as I wrapped my fingers around his girth, and yanked myself away when he shifted. But I wanted to touch him more. I wanted to touch him and not worry about the consequences.

Is that bad? That I touched my brother while he slept? Am I out of order and latching on to him?

My phone buzzes, and I let out a huff when I see who it is.

Parker: Where is it you're going on your trip? Think you can sneak away for a few hours?

Me: I'm eight hours away.

Parker: When do you get home?

Me: Monday. But I'm busy all week.

Parker: I guess I'll see you when I see you.

I shut off my screen and shake my head, looking out the window as the city lights and buildings turn into trees and woodlands.

Malachi sits beside me, all the camping stuff packed into the trunk and sleeping bags rolled up between us. We're going away for the weekend to some spot Dad is desperate to visit in the mountains, and we had no choice but to go too. Family time and all that shit.

You'd think with our parents being rich, with a fancy home and numerous cars, they'd have an RV or at least take the truck to fit all the things into, but nope—Dad wants to try camping the normal way, crushing us with things in the back in the process.

I'm exhausted—I didn't sleep well last night since Malachi went out with his friends and didn't come home until this morning. He climbed into my window at six in the morning, smelling like booze and cigarettes, his eyes bloodshot as he staggered towards my bed.

He turned on my lamp and signed to me, but it was so messy that I didn't understand him. He stood in the middle of my room, swaying and running his hands through his hair in annoyance as he kept trying to communicate with me and failed.

I just helped him out of his hoodie and pants, gave him a glass of water, and slept on his chest while his arms encircled me. He was gone when I woke back up hours later to Dad hammering his fist on my door and demanding I pack for a long weekend of camping.

The. Worst.

My phone buzzes again, and my jaw rolls.

Malachi: *Hold my hand.*

I reread it three times, then glance at him, but he's looking at his phone.

Malachi: *Don't make it obvious.*

Me: *Why do you want to hold my hand?*

Malachi: *Do I need a reason? Give me your hand, or I'll tell Mom you touched my dick while I was asleep.*

I choke on air, and Dad peeks over his shoulder. "Are you okay, angel?"

"Yes," I reply. "Perfectly fine."

Me: *You were awake?*

Malachi: *I'm always awake. Give me your fucking hand.*

Me: Not when they can see.

Malachi shifts beside me, and I glance over to see him pull his flannel off and drop it between us, and my breath hitches as he pulls my hand under the garment and laces our fingers together, our parents none the wiser as my cheeks heat and my throat goes dry.

He squeezes his fingers around mine, and I squeeze back, averting my eyes when Mom turns down the radio. "Did you pack the sandwiches I left on the table?" she asks me.

"Yeah. They're in Malachi's bag."

"And the toilet roll?"

"Yes," Dad says. "We have everything. Stop overthinking."

"But we're so far from home. What if we get an emergency foster?"

"Then we drive back. We'll have a phone signal, so don't start panicking about that either, baby."

He always calls her baby, and it always catches me off guard. I don't remember much of my life before coming to the Vizes, but the name *baby* always makes me uncomfortable, and I think it could be a trigger for me, so I'm glad I don't have memories past being afraid of the dark and the yelling.

Mom sighs then turns to look at my brother. "Where were you last night?"

He stares right through her, not letting go of my hand.

When Mom knows she's not going to get any response, she

rolls her eyes and looks forward again. "It's like talking to a wall sometimes. He wasn't in his room."

She turns again. "Were you out with that blonde?"

I flinch and try to let go of his hand, but he grips me for dear life, ignoring Mom.

"No, he didn't ever go out with her, remember?" Dad reminds her. "She was too afraid of him."

Relief floods through me, and I look over at Malachi, who's studying my reaction.

"You don't need to be an asshole to them," I say under my breath. "Where did you go last night anyway?" I lower my voice. "Before you came to my bed."

I miss the contact as soon as he pulls his hand away and signs, *I was out with my friends. I told you that already.*

Since Dad turns the volume on the radio up, I sign back, *Did you have fun?*

Not really.

Why? I ask.

He smirks and looks away again, pushing his hand under the flannel between us—waiting. His smile grows when I put mine under too, and we hold hands in silence, Mom singing along to an Isabel LaRosa song.

He's typing on his phone again, and mines dings.

Malachi: *You got mad. Why?*

Me: *I don't know what you're talking about.*

Malachi: *Was my baby sister jealous?*

I grimace and shut my screen off—then glance over to see him silently laughing, smiling, his dimples poking inwards.

I mouth, *Asshole*, when our eyes connect.

I'm not sure when I fell asleep, but I jump awake when the car comes to an abrupt stop in the middle of nowhere, and Malachi's thumb is running over the top of my hand, now atop his thigh, the flannel still hiding our hands from Mom and Dad.

We let go, and he signs, *I heard you snoring. Even over Mom's ridiculous singing.*

I narrow my eyes. "I do not snore."

"Yes, you do, angel," Dad says, chuckling.

"It's quite unladylike, dear," Mom adds.

Fuck everyone in this car.

"Okay," Dad starts, unclipping his belt and turning to us, and I sit up straighter. "Malachi, do you want to share with me or your sister? We have two two-man tents."

It's a little weird for him to ask. Why would he share with the dad he doesn't get along with? They don't talk often, if ever, so instead of signing, or even looking up from his phone, he points at me and goes back to typing with his thumb.

"Okay. The kids together. And me and you."

"Why didn't you buy one big tent?" Mom asks.

They then fall into a debate about tents, while I try to look at the group chat Malachi is talking in, but from my angle, I only see emojis and a meme one of his friends has sent.

They're all quite scary to talk to. I picked him up once when he was drunk, and they had heavy metal music playing, their hair spiked up, and piercings all over their faces.

I stood in the driveway in my cheer uniform, and they stared at me like I was the one who didn't fit in. Not like when we were all at school and they were the outcasts.

Malachi punched one of his friends who tried to flirt with me that night—now they all steer clear of me like I'm a disease. He can be quite… violent.

Is it weird that I like it when he's angry and beating people up for me? Except Adam—he did nothing wrong, and he's been very sweet on our dates. Nervous, but sweet. I still have no idea why Malachi attacked him.

Once we have both tents set up, a little fire built between them, and our designated toilet spots organized, we warm up around the flames, darkness falling over us as the stars shine bright. The cracking of the wood fills the silence. Mom has a sleeping bag wrapped around her shoulders; she smiles as she watches me and Malachi try and fail to toast marshmallows on the fire.

His thigh is pressed up against mine, and I'm so aware of it. I wonder if our parents can see it too. But they don't say anything if they do—they just chat between themselves while Malachi helps pick the largest marshmallow and puts it on the end of the stick for me.

"Who wants to take a walk?" Dad asks, and Mom's hand shoots up. "Come on. I think we can get a better view of the stars near the cliff. Are you coming, kids?"

We're eighteen and nineteen, and he still calls us *kids*. We both shake our heads.

As soon as they're out of view, Malachi pulls out his cigarettes and lights one—blows a cloud above our heads and leans his elbows on his parted knees. *You aren't allowed one, so don't ask*, he signs when he sees me looking at the cigarette between his lips.

"I don't want one. Smoking is bad for you," I say, as if he hasn't been smoking for the last two years. "It's like paying to die."

He laughs silently and takes a long drag.

Silence, and then as if something switches within him, he flicks the half-smoked cigarette away and stands. My eyes follow him, and he doesn't give me a second to think or move before he grabs my hand and yanks me to my feet, pulling me towards the tent we're sharing.

I nearly trip up, but his grip on me keeps me on my scurrying feet.

He keeps my hand in his as he unzips the tent, holding it open for me to go in first.

"What's happening?" I ask, glancing around to see if our parents are coming back.

Get in, he signs, *or I'll drag you in.*

I huff and cross my arms, arching a brow at his threat. "No, you won't."

He follows through with the threat as he snatches the front of my sweater and throws me inside, dropping me on the sleeping bag.

"Jesus, Malachi! Do you need to be so damn rough?"

Yes, he signs. *You never listen, stubborn ass.*

"Rude. What are we doing in here? Are you still hungover and need to sleep?"

Maybe he wants to cuddle? He always wants to cuddle to sleep. I don't think I've ever heard of anyone's brother being so needy and constantly having to sleep beside their sister, but then our dynamic changed drastically when he placed my hand on his cock, the same cock I'd ground my ass against—reminding me that I *enjoyed* the forcefulness of him gripping my hand over the impressive length of him.

Oh God. I keep forgetting that happened and then my cheeks get all warm and tingly.

The torch is on, so I can see him lower to his knees in front of me, signing, *Can I see you?*

"You can see me?"

He shakes his head and comes closer, tugging at the collar of my sweater. *Without this.* And then he drops his hand to my thigh, nipping the material. *And these.*

My eyes widen. "Why?" I ask, feeling his breath hit my face from his proximity.

I want to see you, he signs. *I promise not to touch you.*

"I'm sure you've seen plenty of girls without clothes on." I internally groan. Why did I need to sound like a jealous weirdo? "You don't need to see me."

But I pause as he shakes his head. *No.*

"You haven't?"

No, he signs again. *Plus, it's your body I want to see. Why won't you show me?*

I fidget with the zip of the sleeping bag. "What if our parents catch us? You know it's wrong."

They won't. We'll hear them coming.

"But... I'm... Really?"

He blankly stares at me.

"I'm your sister."

And that's your war cry. Take your clothes off, Olivia.

I chew my lip. "I'll do it, but under one condition."

He looks intently at me, waiting.

"We make a game of it." I smile and tip my head, leaning back on my elbows as if my heart isn't about to beat out of my chest. "I ask you questions, and if you answer them honestly, I'll take something off. If you don't answer, or I know you're lying, then you take something off."

Fine, ask me something.

I sit up, hugging my knees. "Did you take drugs last night?"

He silently sighs. *Yeah. Some of my friends were trying it, so I did too.* He plucks the sleeve of my sweater. *Take this off first.*

"I think I get to decide what item of clothing comes off first, thank you very much," I reply, kicking off one of my shoes. "And don't take drugs. They're bad for you—way worse than smoking cigarettes."

He soundlessly laughs.

I wish I could hear it. I'm certain it would be deep and rich. Going by his smile, I just know that hearing it would melt my heart or send me to the woods to slip my hand between my thighs.

"Do you remember how to talk?" I ask. "Like, do you know how to pronounce words and stuff?"

A little. I haven't spoken out loud for a long time.

He rolls his eyes when I kick another shoe off.

"Is your voice deep?"

He tilts his head from side to side. *I think so.*

I slip off the sweater, revealing my tight shirt, and his pupils expand; he's looking at me like he hasn't seen me in just a shirt before. I sleep in a nightdress sometimes, so why is he looking at me like he wants to eat me?

"Can I hear it?" Chancing my luck, I add, "Even just say my name. Or, like, laugh."

No.

I stay still, and he leans in, nudging me with his shoulder. *You need to take something off.*

"You said no, so you take something off."

I answered your question honestly.

I snort a laugh and shake my head, pulling a sock off—he narrows his eyes at me, and I toss the sock away.

"Do you see me as a sister? Because a lot of my friends have brothers and they're... different than what we're like together. I can't imagine them cuddling in bed or playing this game, for example. So, yeah, am I a real sister to you?"

Biting the inside of his cheek, he shifts in place and slips off his flannel, dropping it on top of my sweater. The contrast of my baby pink against his black is like a symbol of us—the innocent cheerleader and the tall, mysterious smoker whose clothes always match his black hair, the person everyone steers clear of or stares at when we're out in public.

When our parents are with us, we do look like siblings who are just opposites, but when we're alone—just me and Malachi—we look odd together.

I gawk at him with uncertainty. "You won't answer my question?"

No. He spins his rings around his fingers then signs, *Your questions are boring.*

I roll my eyes even though my insides are like lava from him refusing to answer my question. Either he thinks it was inappropriate, or he has a secret like me.

"Do you have any piercings?" Silly question, considering his face is clear, his ears have none, and I don't think he has any nipple—

Yes.

I frown, my eyes raking over him. "What? Where?"

He reaches for the back of his neck, snatching off his shirt, messing his hair in the process. He doesn't try to fix it as he throws the shirt at my face. The strong scent of his sandalwood cologne fills my nostrils, and I try not to make it obvious that it drives me a little wild, my cheeks growing hot.

I can't help but let my gaze fall down his chest—the tensed abs from the way he's sitting, the tattoos.

Why are you staring?

I tut. "I wasn't."

Liar.

"Mom and Dad are going to be so weirded out if they walk in and see us."

He shrugs. *Ask me something else.*

His dismissal of the chance of us getting caught is kind of annoying. He might not care about the consequences, but I actually have a conscience and care what they think.

Especially as Mom wants me to choose between Adam and Parker as my suitor. I mean, both are a huge *no*, but I need to pick.

"Why do you want to see me?"

I already told you. I want to look at your body.

My face heats with a blush he can definitely see. "Why? You've seen me in swimwear, and there was that time you walked in on me in the shower." I'd screamed, but he hadn't seemed at all fazed as he'd grabbed one of my towels and leaned against the sink, waiting for me to finish. He had his own bathroom, but we'd just woken up, both of us covered in sweat from our interlinked body parts, and he couldn't be bothered to go to his own room.

I want to see all of you.

Those seven words send my body into overdrive, and my brain short-circuits, blood pounding in my ears. Hesitantly, I pull off my shirt and drop it beside his, hating myself for wearing a sports bra and not some lacy red number that makes my breasts look at least a little better.

He shakes his head. *Another. I answered two.*

The logical thing to do would be to remove my pants so I'm sitting in my underwear, but it seems I'm going down a dangerous path as I pull my sports bra over my head and hold it to my chest.

Give me it, he signs then tries to take the fabric concealing me, but I hold it tighter.

My nipples are hard, and I'm not sure if that's because of the cold weather up in the mountains, or if I'm just heavily turned on that I'm stripping in front of my brother. If I give him my bra, he'll see the stiffness of them, the blush creeping up my chest, and as much as I *want* him to look, I could be calculating this entire game wrong.

He might instantly assume I'm horny and be weirded out. Yeah, he wants to see me, but maybe he's just curious about the female anatomy. Or maybe he's trying to fuck with me.

I read that people with ASPD like to play games with people's heads. Is that what Malachi is doing with me?

"Promise you won't laugh?"

Why the hell would I laugh?

"They… small."

Show me, he harshly signs. *Or I'll make you show me.*

I think I'd like that. "Stop being a caveman."

My sports bra drops onto my lap, and I avert my gaze, keeping it on the torch dangling from the top of the tent, my face most likely going the reddest shade of red—like a strawberry or a tomato.

He's right in front of me, and my breasts are free. My nipples are pebbled, and I'm starting to shake—but I don't think I can blame the cold. I ache between my legs, and as I bring my eyes back to his, I glance down and see the hardness of him through his pants growing more rigid.

His hands are shaking nearly as much as I am as he signs, *Ask me something else.*

I want to cover myself, hike my legs up to hug my knees—something I do a lot when I'm nervous—but I dig my nails into my palms and try to think. My mind isn't working at all, especially with the way his naked chest is rising and falling under the torchlight.

Fucking ask me something, he pushes.

If I ask him something easy, then I'll be nearly naked, so I go deep, knowing he won't answer and will need to remove another item of clothing—maybe his sweats.

My voice betrays me, cracking as I ask, "Why did you attack Adam in the gas station? We were just talking, and you stormed in and went crazy."

He was trying to take what was mine.

"I'm not yours," I reply and regret it instantly as a shadow falls over his face.

"I'm your sister—that's all," I add to make things worse, to anger him further. "We're the Vize kids."

No. You were mine when we were kids, and you're mine now. You'll always be mine.

"Do you see me as a sister?" I ask him again.

Don't cheat your own rules. I already answered a question.

My heart stutters in my chest. "Okay," I whisper.

His nostrils flare, his jaw clenched as his gaze flicks to my pants, and I take a deep breath, hooking my fingers into my waistband and sliding them off, inwardly praising myself for going for a wax with Mom a few days ago.

I'm only in my little pale-pink thong, the straps barely visible against my nude skin. I press my thighs together—the temperature in the tent is rising, and I'm seconds from ruining this game and our relationship and throwing myself at him.

"I think you need to start asking questions," I say, gulping through my nerves. "I'm one answer away from being naked and that's not fair."

He raises his shoulder. *If I asked you to touch yourself, would you?*

Blinking, I crush my thighs together more, caught completely off guard by his question. If I don't answer truthfully, I need to take my thong off, and if I don't answer at all, I'll still end up naked.

The only way for me to see more of his skin is if I'm honest.

I've watched you before, he signs with stiff fingers. *You fuck yourself with your fingers a lot with your curtains open.*

"You've watched me through my window?"

And with cameras in your room.

My eyes ping wide. "You have cameras in my room?"

Yeah. Stop changing the subject. You didn't answer my question. If I asked you to touch yourself, right now, would you?

"First, you'll remove the cameras!"

He shakes his head, and I slap his shoulder.

Answer.

"I think I'd do anything you asked of me," I reply, chewing

the inside of my cheek, hoping I don't sound idiotic. "Under the condition that it stayed a secret."

Oh God. Was that wrong? Oh shitting God.

He's not saying anything—not even blinking as he looks at me.

His silence makes my anxiety skyrocket. Did I say the wrong thing? Was he checking if I wanted him as more than a brother? What if he *is* testing me? What if Mom was right and he is a psychopath and trying to play mind games with me?

But the psycho just said he had cameras in my room and has watched me pleasure myself, so why is this all so confusing?

I reach for my clothes, but he knocks my hand away and gets to his knees, tugging down his sweats over the growing bulge in his briefs, sitting back and kicking them from his inked legs.

Should I be looking at my brother's dick like it's my favorite meal? Probably not.

I lick my lips, imagining the thickness of it sliding down my throat, making me gag as he forces each thrust, silencing my cries, robbing me of air as he slaps me across the face and growls at me to take every inch.

I want him to take, take, take.

"Should we get dressed?"

Not yet, he signs, *and that was another question, which I answered.* I flinch as he hooks his middle finger under the strap on my hip, and a burn sears across my pussy as he rips the underwear from my body.

I gasp. "Malachi!"

He covers my mouth the same way he did when I screamed in his room, but he isn't pressing his body to me this time—he's pushing me onto my back and smacking my legs apart.

Stay still, he signs, shifting so he's kneeling between my legs, his eyes fixed on my pussy, which is soaked and pulsing. I try to close my legs, but he grips them open, glaring at me.

"You said you wouldn't touch me," I say in a soft voice, despite my body turning into an inferno.

Is he going to fuck me?

Am I about to be fucked by my big brother?

Exposed—I'm so exposed and needy and loving that Malachi looks drunk as he places a soft kiss on the side of my knee, making me flinch. *Can I taste you?*

My mouth drops open, heat coursing through my veins. "You said you wouldn't touch me," I repeat, my toes curling slightly from the intensity of his gaze, the place he kissed on the side of my knee sparking all the way to my core.

Then touch yourself.

I stare at him, my mouth opening and closing, and then: "Really?"

Yes.

"You're not trying to mess with me?" I ask. "If you're fucking with me right now, Malachi, I will hit you."

He smirks. *If I'm not allowed to touch you, then you need to do it yourself.*

"What if I say no?" He digs his fingers into my inner thighs, and I let out a shameless whimper. "Okay, okay, okay. But you need to promise not to touch me."

He lifts his pinkie, and I grin as I curl mine around it. "And don't tell anyone. This isn't what siblings do. We'll be in a lot of trouble."

I won't. Our secret, little sister.

I screw my nose up and bat his hands from my legs. "Please don't call me your little sister right now."

He smirks, the dimple indenting deep. *But you are my sister. My dirty little sister who's going to touch herself in front of me. Show your big brother what you sound like when you come.*

All the oxygen in the tent vanishes, and my breath freezes in my chest. My inner walls clench, and I think I'm already soaking from his taboo words alone.

Swallowing my nerves, I slide my hand down my front, parting my legs a little more—Malachi's eyes follow my hand, the way my fingertips attentively part my pussy lips, my back arching as my middle finger dips into my wetness, bringing it up to my clit and circling. The freshly painted red acrylic nail scratches at my tenderness, and I bite my lip.

I've touched myself thousands of times, but having him watching me is making it more intense. I've never been so eager to feel a dick inside me.

I go faster, the coiling sensation at the base of my spine curling around each vertebra, my eyes closing as I lose myself in my own touch and imagine it's someone else.

Someone who shouldn't be watching me.

Someone who should be mortified by me doing this.

My eyelids slide open a little, and Malachi is leaning in, watching me as I pleasure myself. *Can I touch you?*

"No," I pant. "Please don't."

Why?

I sink two fingers inside, ignoring him, dropping my other hand to circle my clit while finger-fucking myself in front of him.

When my eyelids fall open again, my breath hitches as I see his gaze is still glued to my pussy and the way I'm pleasuring myself—grinding my hips upwards as I search for more, but his hand is over his cock through his boxers. I almost want to moan his name, but I stop myself midway and make it sound like a muffled cry.

My inner walls clutch at my fingers repeatedly, and I'm breathing rapidly, a light layer of sweat on my skin. If I tell him to fuck me, will he?

Do I want that?

Would he hurt me?

If I told him that I wanted him to chase me, pin me down,

and take whatever he wanted, against my wishes or not, would he?

Lunacy runs in my veins at this point, because I want my brother to fuck me, and I want him to fuck me hard enough to make it hurt.

The thought alone drives me into an orgasm, and I sink my teeth into my bottom lip as I moan, my back arching off the sleeping bag as I orgasm all over my fingers, throbbing and convulsing beneath him.

I see stars around Malachi, his lips parted, breathing forcefully while he palms himself.

With my fingers still inside me, I pant as I ask, "Do you still want to taste me?"

He nods, and his pupils blow as I lift my glistening fingers to his lips, swiping them across them. He captures my wrist and sucks them into his mouth, my fingers sliding against the warmth of his tongue as he takes them to the knuckles, sucking hard, and I tremble as he bites lightly. If he used his voice, I know I'd hear him hum right now with the way his eyes roll closed, his other hand gripping himself.

My fingers fall from his mouth, and he lunges for me. Before he can catch my lips with his, his body molding over mine, I cover his mouth with my palm. "No," I gasp. "We didn't agree to that!"

His brows knit together, the hardness of his cock poking my

thigh, and he grabs my wrist and pulls my hand from his mouth then snatches my face, attempting to kiss me again, but as his lips layer over mine, I move my head to the side. "No, Malachi."

Yes, Malachi.

Keep going, Malachi.

Take, Malachi.

Why am I like this?

He sits up, pissed off and still hard as a rock, and just when he goes to sign, I sit up too and turn away from him. "Let's just go to sleep," I say, turning off the torch so we're bathed in darkness. "We're obviously not thinking straight."

But the torch is flicked back on, and I freeze when Malachi grabs my throat and pulls me up to my knees in front of him—my airway cut off. There's pressure behind my eyes, and my lungs struggle for air. He releases me, but I stay put, trembling from the orgasm, the fear, and the need for him to *take*.

Don't silence me like that, he signs furiously. *Don't ever fucking silence me, Olivia.*

My brow furrows in confusion. "I... I didn't."

He points to the torch. *I can't fucking talk to you if you can't see me.*

My facial expression softens. "Oh," I say, rubbing my throat. "I'm sorry. I didn't realize I did that. Just... We can't kiss—it's not what siblings do. Regardless of what just happened. Please don't make this awkward."

I don't move away as he yanks me to him by my hair, my breasts pressing to his naked chest.

You used to always kiss me.

"When we were kids, and the kisses were innocent. You… We… No, Malachi."

No? You just— He stops, confused as he drops his hands, not knowing what else to say.

"Mom has me going on dates with guys for me to *marry* them, Malachi. I can't chance being caught kissing you."

You aren't fucking marrying anyone.

As much as I want to really, really kiss him, it would be a colossal blunder. My lips are crackling from the soft brush of his mouth against mine, electricity zapping all over my body from the way he grabbed my face and then my throat, but if I didn't just stop him, we would've made a huge, *huge* mistake.

"We can't," I whisper. "You're Malachi Vize and I'm Olivia Vize. We're sister and brother."

Stop saying that. We aren't blood related. You aren't my real sister, so what's the goddamn problem?

For some reason, those words sting, and my eyes burn as I pull the sleeping bag around my nakedness. "This was a mistake."

"Are they already sleeping?" I hear Mom's voice coming closer, and I rush to grab my clothes and throw them on, Malachi just staring at me, not bothering to put his own clothes on as the footsteps draw closer.

I dive into the sleeping bag in a panic, my heart beating so fast while I pretend to be passed out.

"Are you guys asleep?"

I peek at my brother as she tries the zip—I didn't notice he'd put a small padlock in place to stop it from being opened. Malachi's eyes are on me—I can tell he's mad, even with the torchlight down to the lowest setting and shining on half of his handsome face. His hands are fisted, and his cheeks are red, the rigid length between his legs still masted.

He just tried to kiss me, and I refused him.

I'm already regretting this entire night.

The footsteps leave again. "They must be asleep. Since when are we the ones staying up late? Grab the beers!"

Dad chuckles deeply, and I grimace when I hear them kissing.

Then their tent zips sounds, and silence falls again.

I glance up at Malachi; he lifts his hands then drops them and shakes his head, turning away from me.

CHAPTER 6
OLIVIA

Malachi hasn't spoken to me in weeks.

When he's mad at me, he punishes me by silencing himself around me. When we eat breakfast or lunch or dinner, he won't look at me, and when we go out on family days or nights, he either cancels, or he keeps his face in his phone.

His balcony door is locked every night, and he doesn't sneak into my room at all.

I don't know what to do.

I invited Parker over, thinking he'd at least sneak into my room to strangle him, but I just sat awkwardly next to Parker and pretended to enjoy his company while the cocky wanker spoke about his family business and practically sold himself to me, since he knows I still need to choose between him and Adam.

Malachi didn't show up. If anything, he's been more absent.

Abbi wanted me to go to a party last weekend, but I stayed

home in the hopes that Malachi would get drunk and need me, need me to hold him in bed or even to watch me pretend to sleep—but even though I didn't go out, he didn't come.

My mind likes to play tricks on me. The voices tell me that he regrets what happened in the tent, that he feels disgusted that he watched his sister masturbate before trying to kiss her.

But tonight, my worst nightmare is happening.

Malachi is on a date.

My brother, who's had zero interest in anyone since forever, hasn't ever had a girlfriend or boyfriend, and spends all his time in his room or smoking on his bike or at parties with his friends and taking drugs, is out right now with a girl.

I wouldn't say I was a possessive person, but something about him hugging someone else makes me uneasy. I try to picture him watching someone else fuck themselves with their fingers, and my stomach recoils.

What will they even talk about? Does she know sign language? Will they be able to have a conversation? Will she be nice to him, unlike the way people talked behind his back while he was still in school?

Maybe there won't be much talking…

I bury my head into my pillow to try to banish the image of my brother kissing, touching, or sleeping with someone else. I know he's at an age that he'll be doing that stuff. I mean, he's no longer in high school. I'm about to graduate—people our age do things.

We technically did things.

Things our parents would kick us out for.

I groan to myself and grab my phone, checking my messages from my friends. Everyone is either studying or with their boyfriends. Yet, here I am, in my bed at nine and worrying about Malachi.

I open his messages. He's ignored every single one I've sent since the night in the tent. Even while he lay in the sleeping bag beside me and I texted that I was sorry, he ignored me.

Me: How's your date going?

Then I slap myself on the forehead. He's on a date—why would I message him at all? Mom told me that in confidence, since she saw him looking dressier than usual and asked him where he was going.

He told her he was going on a date, and she was so happy. One, because he'd replied to her for the first time in months. And two, because her son was going on his first date.

I felt sick when she came to my room to tell me with the biggest grin on her face.

I think he told her on purpose. To fuck with me.

But I'm being hypocritical, right? Mom has been forcing me into dates for the past six months with boys who either want their dick sucked or want to get laid.

Getting out of bed, I puff and look around my room. I've

already stress cleaned, my cheerleading uniform is ready, and my gym bag is packed. Even my vanity table is goddamn polished to perfection.

I walk into the bathroom and fill the tub, making sure it's extra bubbly. Then I hunt through my bookcase for something steamy and settle on the monster romance Malachi turned his nose up at when he found it on my bedside unit one night.

I pull off my clothes then sink into the warmth and rest my head against the bath pillow, finding the page I accidentally dog-eared.

An hour passes of me silently worrying about stuff I shouldn't worry about before I get out, wrapping a towel around my body.

With the book back on my shelf, I nearly drop the material from me as I turn around and find Malachi sitting by my open window, his hood up, a cigarette hanging from his mouth. "What the hell?" I whisper-hiss. "You scared me!"

Parting his legs further, he perches his elbows on his thighs, watching me as he puffs.

"Mom is in the next room setting up for the new foster," I point out. "She'll smell the smoke."

Malachi doesn't listen though as he gets to his feet. He inhales a lungful of smoke, his eyes on me, dragging down my body as the orange tip burns bright. My skin heats, and I don't know if it's from the scare I got, or the fact he's like a shadow standing in my dark room, but a wave of tingling excitement

comes over me. I'm reminded of the way he looked at me while
I—

I absolutely cannot feel this way.

Nope. Not towards him.

The night in the tent was a mistake.

"I found your cameras by the way. I threw them in the trash.
Pervert."

Not all of them, he signs.

"What?"

He leans against my window, blanking me, blowing more
smoke out, and I can't help but think about what his night
entailed. Did he kiss her? Touch her? Does he know how to,
considering he has no social skills and rarely tries to communicate
with anyone other than me? He didn't touch me intimately, but
he wanted to, and he tried to kiss me. Maybe he does know?

Dammit, brain.

I close my eyes and press my hand to my forehead. "You
need to go to your own room. I need to get dressed." Then I
drop my hand. "You can't ignore me for weeks then just crawl
back into my life, Malachi. It isn't fair."

Instead of leaving, Malachi inhales another lungful, blowing
it straight at me this time. I don't flinch, even as he takes a step
towards me—but I do gulp harshly as my breath comes out in
bursts.

"I'm not interested in your push and pull anymore. You

can't pick and choose when to speak to me. Take your other hidden cameras, go to your own room, and leave me alone."

The tilt of his head is miniscule, but it's there as he takes another step, causing me to back away. Another, and another, and the back of my knees hit my bed—I sit on the mattress while keeping my eyes on his.

The warmth between my legs is improper—I shouldn't like the way he's looking at me, or the way he comes even closer, his cologne filling my senses and sending my thoughts haywire.

He's not signing; I'm not sure he will either as he pulls down his hood, revealing his messy black hair, then tugs off his motorbike gloves and tosses them on the floor with the cigarette in his mouth. I don't smoke—I hate it—but for some reason, I like it when he does.

He isn't wearing the dressy clothes he left in.

Stubbing the cigarette out on my vanity table, he wets his lips and glances at the bedroom door. I tighten my towel around my body, and for some reason, I say, "It's locked. No one can walk in."

My nipples are hardening under the towel. I can smell the sandalwood on his clothes, mixed with cigarette smoke and the outside air. His cheeks are a little red from how cold it is outside, and I have a sudden urge to wrap my body around his to heat him up.

I'm betraying myself, because I'm mad at him for kicking

me out of his bubble, yet I want him to crawl back into my life—I'd welcome him with open arms and...

But then he pulls off his hoodie, tipping his head towards my pillows.

"You want me to lie down?"

Malachi nods slowly as he kicks off his boots, his eyes not leaving mine as I chew my lip and look between him and the pillow. "I'm in a towel."

You could remove it?

Gulping, I shake my head.

All he does is shrug and move to the opposite side of the bed like he hasn't been a ghost in my life recently—the side he always slept on when he used to sneak into my room to hold me. Sometimes, I used to pretend I had nightmares—I'd either send him a text to come cuddle me until I fell asleep, or I'd go to his room and sleep against his chest, him smelling my hair like it's a drug to him.

Before he shut me out.

Is it wrong to feel like he's betrayed me by going on that date? I don't think any of my friends do that with their brothers.

They definitely don't imagine fucking them.

But for some reason, I don't care. I don't care that it's forbidden to want to lie in his arms and feel the heat from his body—to want to watch him when he isn't already looking at me, to feel butterflies when I hear my window slide up or my door creaking as he pushes through it.

Sick—I'm sick for wanting my brother.

Malachi pulls down the duvet, and I shimmy under it, keeping the towel around me. My bare legs are smooth under the fabric, and my heart thumps as he slips his belt off and pulls down his biker pants, standing in only his briefs.

Mom has music playing next door—"One Way or Another" by Until the Ribbon Breaks is louder than necessary, and she keeps repeating it and belting the words out, probably using a paintbrush as a microphone.

She's so goofy sometimes. I love my mom.

My eyes stay on Malachi, his large presence changing the energy in the room.

I hope he doesn't see how badly he's affecting me—my pulse is hammering, and my mouth is watering as I try to gulp silently. I think there's a puddle between my legs.

I should be mad, but I'm a little blindsided right now. I'll be mad again tomorrow and make him apologize for being an asshole to me for weeks.

My clit aches as I watch his body move. He pulls his shirt off as well to reveal his sculpted torso—the abs he works on every day, the newer ink designs on his chest and shoulder, crawling down his bicep—gilded by the moon shining through my window.

He slips under the duvet and pulls it over us, and I tighten my hold on my towel, even as it opens at the front, exposing me—but he can't see my bare skin. He can't see the goosepimples all over me, and hopefully he isn't some sort of lycanthrope and able to smell my arousal like they can in romance books.

"How was your date?" I ask, hoping there isn't a touch of jealousy in my tone.

Before he can respond with his hands, I shake my head in annoyance and force out more words. "And don't think by me talking to you that I forgive you for being a jerk. If you need to sleep in my bed, fine, but we will talk more about it tomorrow. So, yeah, how was your date?"

You're mad at me, he signs, stating the fucking obvious.

"Not at all," I say sarcastically. "How was your date?"

It was over as soon as it started, he signs, very messily given the way he's positioned. *Why are you mad at me?*

Is he for real? "Because you shut me out after what happened in the tent," I say, a blush creeping up my neck and cheeks. "You said you wouldn't touch me, and you tried to kiss me!" I hiss, throwing my hands upwards and forgetting about my towel. "And then, *poof*, you're gone. Not a word. You haven't come to my room, and it's been really lonely."

I glance at him, seeing the silent chuckle as he grins. "Why are you laughing at me?"

You're cute when you're mad.

A huff, and I cross my arms over the duvet. "What do you

mean by 'it was over as soon as it started'?"

I'm not… His hands freeze, his eyes searching my face before he continues. *Experienced.*

"Liar," I snap. "You didn't seem inexperienced in the tent with me. In fact, you seemed to know exactly what you wanted."

From you, yeah, he signs. *I only felt comfortable doing that with you.*

"Oh," I say, my brows knitting together. "Did you at least kiss her?" The words are like poison on my tongue, and I'm inwardly begging—no… pleading that he didn't. But there's no reason for me to be annoyed if he did. Again, hypocrisy, because I've had to date Parker and Adam.

No, he signs. *I'm not experienced with that either.*

"You haven't kissed someone before?"

He shakes his head, and I sit up, holding the covers to my chest. "But you tried to kiss me."

What part of me feeling comfortable around you don't you understand? Have you kissed someone before?

Debating whether to reply truthfully or not, I decide honesty is key. I nod, and something dangerous flashes behind his eyes. "I don't see why this is a shock to you. Did you forget Mom has been sending me out on dates for months?"

His jaw hardens, and I swear he looks mad for a second before his expression softens. *Can you show me how?*

I blink at him. "Show you how to kiss?"

His chin lowers to his chest slowly in a nod.

"Didn't you hear what I said about the tent situation? I'm your sister," I whisper, remembering Mom is next door setting up the room with the song on a quiet part. "We would get into so much trouble with our parents."

No one needs to know. I kept quiet about what happened in the tent, and all the times we've slept in bed together.

"But it's wrong."

So?

My body burns with anticipation, even though I'm fighting against this. He's so close, and the proximity is creating a heaviness in my lungs as his gaze drops to my mouth before he gradually raises it back to my eyes.

I would only be comfortable with you teaching me how.

"Are you fucking with me right now?"

Smirking, he shakes his head.

"You promise not to tell anyone?"

He raises his pinkie between us, and I sink my teeth into my bottom lip to suppress a smile as my pinkie hooks around his. The touch of our skin sends shocks of electricity up my arm, down my chest, stopping between my legs, and I try to steady my breaths as I keep our pinkies hooked and shift forward, making sure to fix my towel with my free hand to cover myself.

Malachi is a lot larger than me, in both muscle and height, so he always dominates me when we cuddle in bed—he's the perfect big spoon. But this is different. This isn't lying in his arms and fighting my demons, or us watching a movie while his knee randomly bumps into mine, or him carrying me on his back while we jump around the water in the pool or at the beach on vacation.

This is more—I never knew I needed more from him.

I lean up with one straight arm as he rests on his back, so my body is halfway hovering over him. "Are you sure? It doesn't bother you that we're brother and sister?"

Stupid question, considering. He raises a brow in response. *Stop saying that.*

My hair falls around my face, long enough for him to wrap a curl around his finger and tug a little, bringing me closer to him—making my bare legs press against his, sending tingling sensations up my spine and heating my cheeks.

"Remember Mom told us not to kiss on the lips when we were younger? You said we were allowed to because we were siblings, but it got us into trouble. This will, undoubtedly, get us into even more trouble."

He kissed me while sitting at the piano, a soft peck, and it was something we always did, especially at nighttime, before we went to sleep. I always thought it was normal, until one day when we were playing a board game with Mom and Dad, and I pressed my mouth to his while cheering that we won, and our parents lost their shit.

Still, Malachi doesn't give me any sort of reply; he just plays with my hair, bringing it to his nose to inhale the strawberry scent like he always does. He has a fascination with my hair—he always needs to touch it, smell it, play with it.

I know those little interactions are wrong—but it doesn't stop me enjoying them.

He pulls a little harder on my hair, making me lower my body to his, both of us breathing the same air as my nerves kick in. I lick my lips to make sure they aren't dry. "Malachi," I whisper, my body starting to shake. "Are you sure?"

He lifts his hand to the front of his mouth, clamping his fingers together. Sign language for "shut up."

Glancing at my door again, making sure the shadow of our mother isn't lurking and watching us, I shift my hips closer to him, lowering my face and trying not to overthink this.

Malachi's finger stops twirling my hair, and he's holding his breath, the moment dragging in, my mind screaming at me to stop and go at the same time.

I lower more, our noses bumping, then tilt my head slightly and press my mouth to his.

The second our lips touch, the world stops turning, my heart stops beating, and the thoughts telling me I'm twisted, twisted, twisted skid to a halt.

I softly claim his mouth, showing him how to give chaste kisses that aren't like the ones we used to do when we were kids. He copies me. When I kiss his bottom lip, he kisses my top lip gently. I suck on the plump flesh of his bottom lip, tasting the faint hint of his chewing gum and cigarettes, scraping my teeth on it as I pull back to look at him. His pupils have taken over any trace of blue.

"Will I keep going?"

You aren't allowed to stop yet, he signs, his sleepy, hooded gaze flickering to my mouth. *Keep going, little sister.*

Our faces are millimeters apart once more, our noses touching as we fight for air, and I wrap my fingers around his wrist. "Put your hand here," I say, placing it on my cheek. "Or you can put your hands on their hips or in their hair. People like touch, especially while being kissed."

He pulls his hand away and I halt, thinking I've done something wrong, but then he moves both to communicate with me. *What do you like?*

My lips move, but no sound comes out; I'm still on cloud nine from this moment.

The depravity going through my mind right now… I like things that are frowned upon. I have fantasies I return to again and again, and my pursuer always has the same face.

I'm staring right at him.

But then I snap out of it and take his hand again, his eyes following my movements as I place it on my neck, putting pressure over his fingers so they clamp around my slender throat. Enough to make me need to crush my thighs together with how large his hand is, and the way his pupils expand; the sight of him tightening his jaw and narrowing his hold.

"I like to be choked," I admit, feeling miles more comfortable with him than anyone else. "I like rough kisses that hurt."

I let out a shriek as he pushes me onto my back and slams his mouth on mine—his grip on my throat hard enough to stop me breathing and make me see stars behind my eyelids.

My lips part, and he doesn't need any lessons on how to shove his tongue into my mouth, or the way he sucks on mine and devours me. He kisses me like I'm his—like I've belonged to him since I was seven and he was eight. I hum into his mouth, tasting that mint and smoke and *him*. His teeth nip at my lips, stinging, and his grasp gets firmer.

Needing more, I wrap my legs around his hips; my towel creates an annoying barrier between us, but I can still feel the hard length of him pressing against my inner thigh.

He nips my lips more, sucks on my tongue, and uses his free hand to pin my hands above my head, pressing them into the pillow. He captures both in one grip, the other robbing me of air and making the dizziness start to take over.

The number of times I've imagined Malachi doing this when I've been with someone else is embarrassing. Kissing someone but tricking my mind into believing it was my brother, every touch and lick and suck and the way my orgasm rushed through me—it was all for him.

I have an illness. And usually someone would try to treat it, or find ways to help, but the only thing I want is for Malachi to pull his briefs off so I can feel him inside me.

Which is insane, considering this is just practice for him.

As soon as the underside of his cock grazes over my aching pussy, I whimper and fist my hands, sinking my teeth into his lip, hard, and making him bleed—the copper taste filling my mouth.

I moan again, and Malachi pulls back, staring down at me while he keeps sliding his cock against my core. A thin line of blood drips down his chin, and he looks like a psychopath, his eyes burning as he thrusts harder, rubbing against me.

He has to let go of my throat and cover my mouth with his palm to stop me alerting our mom that her son is currently driving her daughter into an orgasm just by dry-humping her through a damn towel.

My eyes roll as he keeps going, and I moan into his hand, meeting each rock of his hips and tensing all over as my high builds, my spine twists, and the coiling sensation burns deep within. I nearly scream as he sinks his teeth into my neck, my ceiling blurring in and out of focus with a mixture of pain, pleasure, and almost passing out from his tight grip.

Before I can reach my orgasm, he flips us again, the towel gliding from my body completely. Naked, and extremely soaked in his lap as I straddle him, I grab fistfuls of his black hair and crush my lips back down on his while his hands explore my body—touching, grasping, caressing my hips as I rock them forward absently.

For being inexperienced, he sure knows how to make me feel like I'm falling from a damn cliff just by kissing me, feeling his hardness through his boxers, searching for the friction that had me oh so close to erupting seconds ago.

His gusts of breath would be audible if he'd never chosen to keep his voice to himself. Each rock of my hip, I feel the silent groans, the gripping hands, and the thickening cock.

He's so reactive to me; everything I do to him, he reciprocates, following my lead as I gasp into his mouth and tug at his wavy strands. He fists my hair at the back of my head, using it to drag me down against him, his fingers slipping to my nape, holding me there.

I should stop—I'm his sister. We're siblings, whether by blood or not, we are the Vize children, and we shouldn't be dry-humping while our tongues tangle, tasting and devouring like we're each other's favorite meal.

But against all the alarm bells ringing in my head, I need more—I *want* more.

His mouth connects with my throat, replacing his hand, and I groan.

"I can show you how to do this," I say, grabbing his hand and pulling it down between us, spreading his fingers then pressing two of them to my clit and circling. He pauses kissing my neck, breaks his mouth from my raw skin, and looks down, watching the way he rubs my sensitive spot.

"Have you done this before?" I ask, because he's picking up the technique really fast, but he shakes his head, watching his fingers.

"Girls love this," I breathe. "Do it while you kiss them. If you do it right, you can make a girl come on your fingers." A whimper pours from my mouth. "Fuck, yes. Just like that, Malachi."

He nods once, twice, wetting his lips as he watches his fingers. Malachi grabs my throat with his other hand and hauls me forward, robbing me of air while his tongue sweeps over mine. His touch isn't gentle—not even slightly. He applies more pressure, circling faster, and I tremble above him while crying into his mouth.

"Faster," I moan. "You're doing so good."

Drool drops from our mouths, landing right where his fingers are driving me insane, making me drenched and circling faster.

"Malachi," I gasp against his lips. "You're making me so wet."

I grind against his fingers as they slide down and over my entrance, soaked and needy and desperate for touch. Malachi lets out a harsh breath, which I can only assume would be a deep moan if he used his voice, as I sink against him, making his fingers edge inside. His cock is still concealed within his boxers but completely tented, rock solid as he pushes another finger inside and thrusts the head of his dick up the crack of my ass.

I want to touch him, but he doesn't need a lesson on how to be touched—he wants me to teach him how to do things to someone else.

The strangled moan I let out is cracked, and as another threatens to spill out, Malachi grips my throat so hard, no sound comes out. Mom's music is at its loudest, and I'm sucking on my brother's tongue while he fucks me with his fingers, his cock rubbing against my ass.

He pulls back, his hands occupied, and he looks like he wants to say something to me, but when he releases my throat, he struggles to sign with one hand, so he grits his teeth and jerks my mouth back to his by grabbing the back of my head. The force of it has my palm slapping the partition wall above his head, making the surface shake and one of my picture frames fall to the ground.

"Fuck," I pant. "Keep going."

I freeze as a knock sounds on the door a minute later. "Sweetheart? Are you okay in there?"

I try to get off Malachi, but he holds me in place by the hair, pushing me back enough that he can capture one of my nipples in his mouth while sinking his fingers in to the knuckles and curling them just as he sucks—hard.

All I can do is bite my lip, splitting the skin to stop myself from crying out.

She knocks again and jiggles the handle, my heart stuttering in my chest as he moves to my other nipple, sinking his teeth in enough to make it sting—yet the pain makes me wetter, the taste of my own blood in my mouth mixing with his fingers fucking me, his cock rubbing against my ass—I explode.

I come all over his fingers as the coiling at the base of my spine blows, black spots behind my eyes as my pussy grips his fingers over and over, my nipples hard in his wet mouth, tight, and painful as I ride my orgasm to its pinnacle.

Malachi pops my nipple from his mouth and softly kisses me, leaving his fingers inside while I spasm around them, clutching at them with each pulse. His tongue slips into my mouth, and I kiss him back. It's slow, sensual, and I keep pausing to try to breathe.

I push against his chest and lean back, putting a little distance between us as I pant—him watching me with a drunk gaze and puffy lips from kissing me.

"No, I think she's snuck out with Parker. I'll be calling his parents to tell them that we're setting them up for an arranged marriage, not to fuck around at all hours. Plus, she was with Adam last weekend, remember? I had to go get her the morning-after pill." Silence, and then… "Is Malachi in his room?"

"I'll go check," my dad says, and my eyes widen.

I roll away from him and jump out of the bed, snatching my towel up. "Go!" I mouth, pointing to my window. "Hurry before Dad gets to your room."

Everything within me heats all over again as Malachi sucks his fingers into his mouth while rising from the bed and walking towards me.

Why did you need the morning-after pill? he signs.

When I stay silent, he pushes me until my back hits the wall. *Fucking answer me!*

My body rattles as I hug myself, covering my breasts. He hadn't spoken to me in weeks, so when would I have had the chance to tell him that our parents arranged for me to sleep with Adam? Or that I had no choice but to go along with it?

I didn't refuse—I didn't feel like I could. He didn't even want to do it—he doesn't like me that way, but when we said we'd pretend, his maid overheard and ratted us out, so we'd been forced to have an audience.

He wasn't my first.

Parker was. Dad's business partner's entitled, pain-in-the-ass son—offered no argument when they told us to go to the room together. In fact, he asked for money first, and Mom being Mom, she paid him to take my virginity.

Malachi has no idea about any of this; all he knows is that I'm going to be shoved into a marriage set up by our parents.

I love my parents, but I also hate them.

He steps back and snatches his shirt from the ground, pulling it on, then signs, *Will I go out there right now and ask them why you needed a plan B?*

I take a deep breath. "They wanted me to sleep with him to prove my loyalty."

What?

If I mention they did the same with Parker, he might go out there and lose his shit. "Don't look at me like that. You know what they're like when it comes to me being partnered up with some wealthy asshole. I wasn't going to tell them no, Malachi," I hiss. "I don't have that luxury."

His jaw tenses sharp enough to cut through leather. His lip is swollen at the side from me biting it, and I can feel my own lump from his nipping mine, and I want to go back to two minutes ago, because now he's mad. His eyes flick to the door, his knuckles cracking.

Was Adam your first? The one who made you realize you liked to be choked?

My mouth drops open. "No," I reply.

No to which part, Olivia?

Malachi looks like he wants to murder me.

You fuck him again, or anyone else, and I'll kill them.

"I'm supposed to marry one of them," I argue.

He eats up the distance between us, and I flinch, readying for him to hit me for the first time ever, but he just tucks the stray strands of hair behind my ears and presses a firm kiss to my lips before grabbing the rest of his clothes and disappearing out the window.

I take a second to breathe, my nerve endings still on fire, barely able to walk straight as I kick his motorbike gloves under my bed and hold the towel around me.

Unlocking the door, I open it enough to pop my head out, making sure to make myself known so she doesn't actually call anyone's parents. "What's wrong?" I ask, rubbing my eyes.

Mom turns and presses her hand to her chest, paint splashed over her face from decorating. "Oh, I thought something was wrong. I heard a bang."

I rub my eyes some more. "I just woke up."

She smiles, and I feel bad for lying to her—for coming all over her son's fingers two minutes ago.

"Go back to bed, sweetie. I'll make some breakfast in the morning before you have practice."

I nod. "Night, Mom."

"Night."

CHAPTER 7
OLIVIA

Breakfast is quiet—Dad is trying to talk to us about his working week and telling Malachi he needs to sort his shit out so he can take over his law firm. My brother ignores him and watches me while I eat.

Parker and Adam are brought up twice, because I've yet to choose, and both times, Malachi fists his hands and glares at his cereal.

I can still feel his fingers inside me. I keep staring at his hands, the veins, the muscles of his arms as he stretches them above him and cracks his neck.

Mom goes to work on the room beside mine again, and Dad goes to his office, leaving me and Malachi alone at the breakfast table.

He taps his bowl with his spoon, filling the silence, before I clear my throat. "Don't get mad at what I'm about to say."

My brother looks up at me and drops the spoon in his bowl,

folding his arms in front of himself and arching his brow slightly.

"I'm staying at Parker's place tonight."

Why?

"Mom arranged it." I rub my hand down my face in exasperation. "There's no reason for you to be looking at me like I shit in your cereal either. I was only teaching you last night so you'd know what to do, and feel comfortable doing it, when you go on your dates. That's where the lessons end because you're obviously a natural."

They end when I say they end, he signs.

I roll my eyes. "You're unbelievable."

Come to my room.

"No," I scoff. "Why would I do that?"

Because I want you to show me… He stops and smirks. *I want you to teach me what it's like to have lips like yours around my cock.*

I stutter, nearly choking on my cereal, stuck and dry in my throat. "Jesus, Malachi."

"What did he do this time?" Mom asks, and my spine stiffens. "Are you annoying your sister again? Shouldn't you be fixing the bike you crashed last night and didn't tell anyone about?"

My eyes flicker to him, and he ignores Mom. *I meant what I said,* he signs, kicking his chair back and standing, before tossing the bowl into the sink and walking off.

We have staff in the manor, but they keep themselves busy. The cleaner—I refuse to call her a maid—hates when we leave stuff in the sink.

Mom puts her hands to her hips. "What was that about?"

I shrug, shoving a spoonful of cereal into my mouth. "Is the room nearly ready?"

She goes into a spiel about décor, and the way she wants the furniture to be arranged, and starts showing me pictures on her phone.

When she gives up and goes back to painting, I check my own phone.

Malachi*: Waiting.*

Me*: Bite me.*

Malachi*: I already did. Move it, or I'll come down there and drag you up here.*

I glare at my phone, fed up with his hot and cold. He just spent weeks blanking me, so he can have the same damn treatment. I call Abbi and ask her to go to the mall, then I run to my room, get dressed, and head down to the garage—but before I can climb into my car, Malachi grabs my plait and slams me against it.

I don't have a second to think before he kisses me. There's no romance, no cuteness, just him ravaging me like he's a starved man while pulling my hair nearly from the roots. He slips his tongue past my lips and moves it against mine, grabbing the back of my knees and lifting me into his arms, slamming me against my car again.

He grinds against my core, already hard, his fingers digging into my ass.

"Malachi," I breathe as he tugs my hair again. "Cameras."

If dad were to look at the security system, he'd see his kids kissing, devouring each other like starved animals.

He breaks away from my mouth and pulls my hair to the side, tilting my head and sucking on my pulse beneath my ear so harshly, I know he'll leave a mark.

I kick my legs out, shoving against his chest, and after a long minute of fighting him, he moves his mouth down my chest, snatching my shirt down to take my nipple into his mouth.

My eyes roll, and I stop fighting, my pussy aching for his touch again as I relax in his arms, moving my hips to rock against his cock. I like that he didn't stop when I pushed at him; he only sucked my skin harder and gripped me more painfully, and it... excited me.

Sick, sick, sick.

My phone rings, and he pulls back, breathless.

"You don't need any more lessons on kissing," I say, panting, feeling him pressed into me. "Or how to suck on a nipple. Put me down."

Begrudgingly, he does, and I wipe the back of my hand across my mouth while steadying myself.

Teach me more.

I roll my eyes and open my car door. "Fine. But stop being

a dickhead to me."

I sneak out of my window, two hours before Parker's due to pick me up, wearing a little dress that doesn't need a bra underneath. It's raining, so the ledge to his balcony is slippery.

I reach the balcony without falling to my death and find him watching me, leaning against it with a cigarette. He smirks when I try to climb over and slip, reaching his hand for me to grab. I throw my leg over, and he catches me, pinning me to the stone balcony by his hips.

I glance around, but the place is in darkness.

"I don't have long," I say. "What do you want me to teach you?"

He shrugs. *Whatever it is you like.* He blows smoke above my head and flicks the rest of his cigarette off the balcony.

I laugh. "If you want to learn what I like, then being in a bedroom isn't that. You want to chase me around a cemetery? The woods? Make me terrified while you fuck me?"

His pupils expand. *If that's what you want.*

"But not everyone likes that," I say, curling my fingers into the waistband of his shorts. "Some people like to be serenaded, pleasured with love and words full of meaning."

I reach into his shorts, under his briefs, and his jaw tightens as I wrap my fingers around his cock. "Some people like to take things nice and slow, Malachi, because it builds trust." I stroke him, and he grows in my palm. "Do you want me to teach you slow?"

He shakes his head, thrusting into my hand, his chest heaving.

"Do you want me to show you what I look like on my knees?"

He nods, and I hum, twisting my wrist as I reach his engorged head, faltering when I feel the faint piercing there. More than one actually.

"Did they hurt?" I ask him, tracing my fingertip up the metal bars on the underside of his cock. Like a ladder to the tip.

No, he signs. *Knees. Now.*

I smile as I let out a puffed laugh. "Make me."

He grits his teeth, eyes searching my face as I graze my fingers over the head of his cock again, then snatches my throat, slams his mouth on mine for a brief kiss, and shoves me down to my knees. The balcony is wet, the rain pattering down, soaking my hair and my dress, but I don't care.

The forcefulness makes my pussy throb with need as I settle my ass on my ankles, looking up at him. His soaked hair drips down onto my face before he runs his fingers through it, making it stick up in all directions while he tips my chin with one hand and pulls his cock out with the other.

"I want to taste you," I say, my tone breathy and erotic. "I want to go to Parker's house, and when I kiss him, I want him to taste you on my tongue."

Angering him is stupid, but I love seeing the darkness taking over his eyes, the roughness of his grabbing my hair and making me open my mouth. I stick my tongue out, licking the tip of his dick and making it jerk in front of me.

His precum is leaking from him, and I lean up on my knees enough to wrap my lips around the head, tasting him, feeling the metal rub against my bottom lip—letting out a moan as his fingers tighten in my hair as I suck lightly.

I pop it back out of my mouth, running my hands up his thighs. "Does it feel good?"

With one hand, he strains as he signs, *Yes.*

"You're so big. I don't think I'll get it all in my mouth." I drag my tongue from base to tip, feeling the ridges of his piercing and wondering how they'll feel if he ever fucks me.

He lets go of my hair. *I'll make it fit. Even if it hurts.*

It's the only warning I get before he snatches my hair and forces his cock into my mouth, nearly knocking me over. The bluntness against the back of my throat has me nearly choking, gagging, but I adjust my throat and swallow around him as he starts thrusting into my mouth like a madman.

It does hurt, but the heat starts coiling at my core from how rough he's being—robbing me of air, my scalp burning from the grip in my hair, my eyes watering.

He throws his head back as he fucks my mouth, growing thicker and nearly crushing my throat. Thrusting, pushing further down my throat, pulsing as even more precum leaks out.

I dig my nails into the back of his thighs, pulling him closer to me even though I need space to breathe. He pants inaudibly, dropping his head down to watch me, releasing one hand from my hair and pinching my nose.

My eyes widen, my clit throbbing as my lungs start to seize. I can't breathe. I can't do anything but let him fuck my mouth.

"Malachi!" Dad yells, and he stills, keeping his cock deep in my throat as I gag. He leans over the balcony, but I can't see. "Take whoever that is into your goddamn bedroom! Jesus Christ!"

Malachi looks down at me, grinning as he pulls out a little for me to gasp in air, then fucks into my mouth again. He signs, *I wonder what he'd think if he knew his precious daughter was the one sucking his son's cock like the filthy little fucking whore she is.*

One more thrust, and his cock swells as his eyes roll to the back of his head, Dad still shouting down in the yard, but he keeps going until he stills, the warm liquid hitting the back of my throat as his dick twitches in my mouth.

He pulls out completely, and snatches my jaw, keeping my mouth open. With my tongue out, he stares at his cum pooling in my mouth, capturing some of it spilling from the corner with his thumb and wiping it across my lips.

My eyes widen as he slides two fingers into my mouth, forcing them to the back of my throat and making me gag and swallow every drop.

I fall forward, gasping in the rain, filling my lungs as he steps away. I look up to see him tucking his dick away. *Go kiss your future husband, little sister. And when you do, you better think about me and all the ways I'll fuck you in his blood.*

Parker sits beside me, his friends all laughing and drinking around us on the sofas. We're in one of their basements, and what should have been a date has turned into him guilt-tripping me into being here, since I was making him miss out on a good night.

I did try to go home, but he insisted I go with him, mentioned his old man would be mad at him if he fucked me off for a party.

He's taken four lines so far, and his friends are all idiots.

His arm is behind me, his fingers grazing my shoulder, and I'm very aware of his intentions. He's a fuckboy—known for being the type of guy to sleep around and get praised for it. His shaggy blonde hair falls over his eyes, so he keeps needing to bat it away to see, and he smells like vinegar. I don't think he's even showered after working out.

With that cocky attitude, you'd think he'd at least be good in bed, but I was bored to death, trying not to fall asleep while I stared at the ceiling the entire time.

This is the guy Mom paid to fuck me. My father's business partner's idiotic son. My potential future husband.

Yack.

I have no interest in him—I'd rather kiss a poisonous frog. Or maybe Malachi's spider Spikey?

No.

Honestly, I want to yell at my parents for forcing me into these arrangements. Not only is he five years older than me, but he also keeps calling me "kid," even when he was inside me. He's kissed me twice, and I felt like I was making out with a lampshade.

No sparks whatsoever. But then again, I have been kissing Malachi.

Parker's voice slithers near my ear. "You want to go to one of the rooms?"

I should say no, but he might tell my parents I'm not being cooperative, so I unenthusiastically nod.

One of his friends stands. "Parks!" he cheers. "Think your girl will suck me off?"

He laughs. "Probably. She's easy enough."

My face falls, and I pull away from him. "What the fuck?"

Faking a pout, he nips my chin. "Don't act all innocent. I bet if I told you to, you'd suck every single one of us off."

I scoff and cross my arms, trying to feign confidence even though my bones are shaking with fear. "I don't think so." Then I turn and head for the basement door. "I'm going home."

A hand knotted in my hair stops me. "I have three more hours with you, so do as you're fucking told."

Parker spins me round and slaps me across the face with the back of his hand, sending a searing burn across my cheek. My hair falls over my face, and I look up at him.

He just… hit me.

I gulp down my anxiety, not daring to throw anything back at him. I'm not stupid. He's way taller, and the rest—all ten of them—start to laugh at me. All drugged and drunk and watching me like I'm some whore they paid to fuck.

"Unless you want the world to know your mom sold your virginity to me for five grand, I'd open those pretty little lips of yours and stick out your tongue," Parker whispers against my ear. "Sit your pretty ass down while I grab us drinks."

My eyes water, and when Parker and his friends all go grab more drinks, I climb back onto the sofa and slide my phone out, opening Malachi's contact details and sending him my location.

Screw the consequences.

The location is received, and I don't have time to send anything else, not even a warning that there are loads of them here, before Parker sits back down beside me.

"Are you out of your little mood?"

I accept the beer, but I don't drink it. "You just offered me up to all your friends."

"Yeah, I did. Is that a problem?"

I grit my teeth and stare forward, flinching as he brushes hair from my shoulder. "I asked you a question, Olive."

"My name is Olivia."

"It doesn't really matter what your name is though, does it?"

My chest heaves as I watch the clock. Malachi knows I'm out with Parker—he made sure his cum was coating my mouth and throat before I left, kissing me harder than ever before to prove a point. When I got to Parker's, he forced his mouth on mine, and the only positive was that he would've had my brother's taste on his tongue.

Asshole.

There's a disturbance outside the basement door, and Parker sits up straight to see, but someone comes smashing through it, knocking the door off its hinges, and everyone jumps to their feet as five masked men walk in swinging bats.

I feel myself smile as the one in the middle, his face covered with a balaclava, twirls the silver bat between his fingers. Malachi's eyes find me, and he tilts his head towards the broken doorway, telling me silently to get out.

I run without giving it a second thought, shrugging off

Parker's hand when he reaches for me.

I stop beside Malachi, whose gaze is now fixed on Parker. "Thank you," I say. "He was going to make me blow him and his friends."

Parker lifts his hands as Malachi raises the bat and storms towards him. "Hey, man. She's a goddamn liar! She——"

He's silenced by the bat smashing into the side of his face, knocking him sideways.

I run out of there just as I see my brother grab Parker by the hair and punch him hard in the nose, breaking it instantly.

"Olivia? Malachi?" Mom's panicked voice reaches my ears as the front door opens, gentle, bloody hands on my shoulders as my brother walks me in. "Jamieson! Jamieson! Malachi is covered in blood!"

Heavy footsteps, then I hear my dad. "What the hell happened?"

"The next time you pair me up with someone, make sure he isn't a piece of shit," I snap at her. "Parker and his friends were going to attack me. He said that if I didn't agree to it, he'd tell the world you paid him to take my virginity."

Mom presses her hand to her chest. "Did he hurt you?"

My chin trembles as tears slip down my cheeks, and I shake my head. "I sent Malachi my location, and he got to me before they could do anything. Him and his ten friends were going to—" I stop, my stomach twisting. "Don't ever pair me up with someone like him again."

"*Ten of them?*" Dad shouts. "That piece of shit."

But then Malachi's burning, fuming gaze lifts to Mom, as if it just hit him what I said. *You paid someone to fuck my sister?*

It takes her a second to realize he communicated with her. "Don't speak like that," she scolds. "And I did it to help you, Olivia. I never intended for him to attack you."

Dad steps up beside her, glaring. "Wait. Did I hear that right? You paid Parker fucking Melrose to sleep with my daughter?"

"He said no to the arrangement! I had to make him say yes! She was a virgin, and he didn't want someone innocent!"

Dad's jaw ticks, his nostrils flaring the same way my brother's do when he's mad. "I'll speak to you later about this."

He gives me a warm smile. "I'm going to fix this, angel. No one tries to hurt my child and gets away with it." He walks away, shouting over his shoulder, "Malachi, grab your baseball bat and meet me in the garage."

"Oh, he already got them."

Dad stops, turning. "What?"

"They're all dealt with."

I got them, Dad, Malachi signs, and my eyes widen. He never talks to him. Ever. Never mind calling him Dad. It hits my father, and I can tell he wants to hug my brother, but he won't.

"Good one, son. If any cops show up, I'll deal with them." He gestures to the stairs. "Go shower. You're covered in blood, and it's staining your mother's carpets."

A short while later, I stand in the shower and let the water roll down my body, listening to "In Flames" by Digital Daggers down low from my little speaker.

Malachi is sitting against my sink, silently watching me. His knuckles are all split open and bleeding, and he keeps fisting his hands and rubbing his face as he shakes his head. He broke Parker's legs with his bat and shoved the handle of the bat down one of the other's throats, dislocating their jaw and making them vomit blood.

His friends got the rest.

I don't think any of them will bother me again.

Parker's definitely not going to be reaching out anytime soon. Even Dad had a go at Mom for the secret money slip, until she cried and apologized.

The agreement with Parker's family is over—I'll probably be forced to marry Adam.

Stupid.

At least I know Adam wouldn't ever hurt me. He's too delicate and soft; even when I had to sleep with him, he was shaking so badly and apologizing over and over because he couldn't get hard.

I don't want to get married—ever.

My brother slides open the shower door and climbs in. My eyes follow him as he soaks his hair under the water, and I gasp at the blood streaming from his black hair.

It's not mine, he signs. *I'm not sure whose blood it is. The place was a bloodbath.*

"You know…" I start, clearing my throat as I glance down at his shorts, which are getting soaked by the shower. "Usually people shower naked."

He blinks then stares at me as he continues rubbing the blood from his hair and the back of his neck.

"How exactly did you get so much of someone else's blood in your hair?"

It got messy, he signs. *Are you alright?*

I shrug. "Shit happens. I should've known not to go there."

He tilts his head, frowning. *You know none of that was your fault, right?*

"I kind of put myself in that position by going there. If I hadn't got my location to you…"

He sighs silently. *Forever blaming yourself for shit. And you aren't going out with anyone else. Tell that other dude to fuck off.*

"I'm afraid that's not your decision, big brother."

He groans and closes his eyes, signing, *Don't call me that right now.*

"Why?" I ask when he keeps his eyes closed.

Because I want to do things to you, and you calling me that makes me want to do even dirtier things to your mouth.

My mouth closes, and I stop breathing. He gets turned on by me calling him my brother? Is that… allowed? Wrong?

I don't think I really care.

"Do you even need lessons anymore? You seem like a natural."

He doesn't respond, rubbing soap on his chest and licking his lips as he frowns at me.

"Or…" I stop, sliding my hand up his chest, layering it over one of his and feeling his pounding heart. "I could teach you something I really want you to do to me."

He nods, and I slide my hand up to his shoulder, keeping my eyes on his as I apply pressure, pushing down, and when he tilts his head, I say, "Get on your knees for your little sister, Malachi."

His cock jerks between us, hitting against my navel, and I quirk a brow at his silence.

One at a time, he drops to his knees, my hand still on his powerful shoulder, taut with the muscles he's been building since he was sixteen. I cup his jaw, holding his chin, then I lean down and press a kiss to his mouth. "I want you to taste me," I say against his lips. "I want your mouth on me. Do you want me to teach you?"

His lips part, pupils expanding as he nods. I don't think he's even breathing.

I straighten, and his darkening eyes are on me, dropping down to my navel as his palms slide up my thighs, the water running all over my body like a fountain.

He's waiting for instructions, the clueless look in his eyes making me giddy—Malachi Vize, innocent only for me, on his knees for his sister, looking like I own him.

I *do* own him.

"Use your tongue first," I say, parting myself with my fingers to show him my clit. "Right here. Lick me."

My brother's blue eyes burn into my soul as he brings his face closer to my parted pussy, his warm breath hitting me and making me tense all over. He flattens his tongue against my clit, and I release my lips to slam my palms on the wall on each side of me.

Keeping myself upright on shaky legs, I glance down as he swipes his tongue against my folds, sucking them lightly. Licking from entrance to clit slowly, he has me tensing with each flick of his tongue, the tip slipping against my entrance.

He eases back, and I already miss his mouth on my pussy. *Am I doing it right?*

"Yes," I breathe. "God, yes. So good, Malachi. Keep doing it, and suck on my clit too," I whisper, putting my hand on the back of his head and guiding him back to my pussy.

He smirks, but barely—and I'm thrown back into bliss as he buries his face between my legs, only giving my clit attention with licks and sucks and the faint graze of his teeth. His fingers are digging into the backs of my thighs, bruising them most likely, as he sucks my clit into his mouth and swirls his tongue around it.

I open my legs wider, my mouth gaping on silent cries, my back sinking against the shower wall, as I ride his tongue, desperate for the warmth of it to push deep into my pussy. For him to stand up and fuck me.

I brush my fingers through his black hair and pull, using my hold as leverage to fuck his face, whimpering as his tongue nearly enters me—but he keeps focusing on just my clit, and I want more.

"Stick your tongue out," I order him, and he glances up at me through his long and thick dark lashes, doing as I tell him. I move against the rigid tongue, and when it enters me slightly, I need to cover my mouth to muffle the moan as Malachi understands what I want and forces his tongue inside me, sucking and devouring and thrusting it in and out as he cups my ass with both hands, parting my pussy from the other angle.

"You're going to make me come," I moan. "Keep going. You're doing so well, Malachi."

This pushes me more, and as his fingertips part my back hole, he alternates between sucking my clit and fucking me with his tongue.

I reach behind me, down to my ass where his hands are, and gasp as my body starts to light up, my nerve endings sparking, my eyes rolling.

"Use your fingers," I order—and nearly scream the manor down as he pushes a fingertip into my back hole instead of my pussy, but I don't stop him.

I ride his face and finger as it eases in and out, going deeper as I push against the back of his hand, moaning aloud and not caring if our parents can hear us.

"You're doing so well, Malachi," I praise, grabbing his other hand and wrapping my fingers around two of his. "Push these inside my pussy while you suck my clit. Fuck both of my holes with your fingers."

His teeth graze my clit as he pushes two fingers inside, just as the other finger slips back into my ass—and I cover my mouth on a scream as everything smacks into me.

The orgasm my brother draws out of me has me rolling my eyes, barely able to stand as my knees buckle through the intensity. He's holding me up by pushing us both against the wall, still fucking both ends with his fingers and sucking on my clit so harshly, I think he might bruise that too.

I grind against his mouth with each pulse, each grip of my inner walls around his fingers, and he licks up my juices as he slowly slips his fingers free. I flinch as he forces his tongue inside me again, sucking and swallowing me, not once taking his eyes off me.

His bottom lip drags from my entrance, all the way up and over my clit, stopping at my navel. *Good?*

I blush at the way he's smiling up at me, the light in his eyes returning, his hands lowering to clamp delicately at my thighs to keep me up, still on his knees as the water soaks him. His lips are raw, and as I nod and grin, leaning down to kiss him, I yelp as he drags me down to the shower floor and kisses me until we're even more breathless.

I end up on my knees again, feeling his piercings with the flat of my tongue as I swallow his cock, and he pounds into my mouth with a painful grip of my hair.

He spills into my throat, not my mouth, and I swallow every drop before we get out of the shower, kissing against the sink wrapped in towels, his hands holding my face as he tilts my head to kiss me deeper, hungrier, biting at my lips and tongue until we're both dry. Then he carries me to bed and drops me on the mattress, and I giggle.

He bends down to kiss me. The annoying part of my brain has me lifting my hand to stop him, pressing my fingers to his lips.

His brows knit together. *What's wrong?*

"I'm scared that if we keep doing this, I'll start falling for you. And we… me and you… it's impossible."

He sits on the edge of my bed. *These were just lessons for you.*

Not a question—a statement. One that might have been true months ago when he asked me to show him how to kiss, but now? I can't even think about anyone else without his face, his hands, his body infiltrating my mind.

"Were they more for you?"

I don't know, he signs, and he genuinely looks dumbfounded. *I don't understand the way I feel. It's different. Like I don't have any control.*

His diagnosis comes to mind, and I reach for his hand. "Maybe we should stop before it gets more confusing. Would you be comfortable with someone else now that we've... done things, or do you still want lessons?"

Can I not just be comfortable with you?

"I'm your sister."

And?

I snort a laugh. "Do you want to give Dad a heart attack?"

He gives me a look that says he absolutely does want to do that—then I pull him into bed with me, and we kiss again, completely exhausted as we both fall asleep.

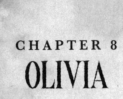

CHAPTER 8
OLIVIA

Before I go to cheer, Mom wants me to go shopping with her to buy furniture for the new foster—a five-year-old girl called Molly. She was taken from her mother after doctors found drugs in the little girl's system. The parents were given many warnings, but they didn't even try for the sake of their child.

My dad was given her case when the father was being charged for raping his wife—and Jamieson Vize being Jamieson Vize knew he had to save the girl with a story nearly identical to my own.

She joins the family next week.

Malachi doesn't care—he hates children and will probably stay far away from her. The past three months have been… fun. When we aren't sneaking into bed and continuing our "lessons," we're hiding in places around the house while either one of us practices our oral skills or kissing until we're satisfied.

Which is never.

Mom has given me some freedom, if I can even call it that. Adam is the one she wants me to marry now Parker is out of the picture, but she told me to take a year before the arrangement goes ahead. So I can enjoy the "single life" until I inevitably become Mrs. Adam Peckham.

Me being the great daughter I am, I agreed.

Malachi isn't happy about it at all; that much is clear from the way he glares at Mom whenever she's around, and even Dad had been keeping his distance from her since he found out about her secret payoff she gave to Parker.

He's done nothing but apologize to me. He tells me he'd never sell his daughter's virginity and that he's contemplating divorcing Mom for her actions, but he still loves her, so he won't. Not that I want them to separate.

"I'm going to Abbi's tonight," I announce. "She's having a little party for her nineteenth."

My brother's eyes slowly lift to me, and he shakes his head. *No.*

I screw my nose up. *Don't dare try telling me what to do*, I sign back while Mom's back is turned. *I'm staying there, and you won't stop me.*

I will.

I scoff and shake my head. *Fuck you.*

I'll do that too.

The blush on my cheeks betrays me, and I kick him under the table, making him cough through a laugh while he eats his cereal. *Just being honest, little sister.*

I'm fed up with everyone running my life, so I glare and blank him and grin at my mom. "Can you drop me off? I don't want to have any drunken urges to drive home under the influence later."

Malachi straightens. He doesn't like it when I go out drinking. We're not going *out* out, since we're not twenty-one and don't currently have fake IDs, but it's so easy to get booze for house parties.

"Of course, sweetie. Have you decided where you want to go for your nineteenth? We could go camping again, or maybe Florida? Oh, wait, did you not say you wanted to visit Europe?"

"Maybe Paris," I say, tilting my head from side to side. "I'll ask Abbi to come with us."

Once I finish eating, I head up to the second floor to go through my mom's walk-in closet, hunting for the shoes she stole from me. I click on the light and jump when I see someone standing behind me in the reflection of the mirror.

"Dammit, you idiot! Don't sneak up on me like that!"

Malachi leans his shoulder against the door frame. *We should do more lessons. We've been stuck on the same one for months.*

Popping my hip out, I cross my arms. "Because you said you wanted to stay on oral for a little while longer for *extra practice.*

Honestly, you don't need any more lessons. I'm sure you can navigate the rest on your own." I smirk at the rage taking over his eyes. "It's more of an instinct thing from here on out. Your wooing sexual skills are… fine."

He narrows his eyes and takes a step into the walk-in closet, making my nerves tingle. *Fine*, he signs, raising a brow. *Just fine?*

To be an asshole, I smile. "Yep. Now fuck off. I'm busy, and you're the last person I want to converse with after telling me not to go to Abbi's tonight. What's with that anyway? You think you can get me on my knees then tell me what to do in my life?"

Malachi rapidly eats up the distance between us, and my stance falters as my back hits the wall, trying to keep him as far away as possible. Mom and Dad are home—they could easily walk up the stairs and see us. It might not have stopped us before, loving the thrill of being caught, but I'm trying to be mad at him, and I want to stay mad.

Does that stop him though? No, of course not—he leans in, bringing his nose just above my ear to inhale the scent of my hair while his cologne distracts me. Always smelling my hair, always rubbing it between his fingers. The tip of his nose grazes the shell of my ear, and I tense all over as he nips my lobe between his teeth. My pussy throbs, and I know my mood is about to vanish, and the next lesson might commence at any moment.

He bites lightly, and I tilt my head to the side to give him more access, elongating my throat so he can kiss down the expanse of it and suck my skin in that way that has me shaking, hot waves of pleasure throbbing between my legs.

His tongue licks against my pulse, and I feel it pump erratically as his hand takes my hip, pinning me in place while his other hand slips under my cheer uniform, gentle touches against the soaked material. I can see the words in his eyes. *So wet, little sister.*

My lips part on a moan as he applies pressure to my clit, but it's gone as soon as he does it—he pulls his hand away, caressing his palm against my chest, between my breasts, over my heart, probably feeling it nearly bounding from my ribs. It's beating like a drum for him. Hard thumps, matching my pulse, and he holds it there as he captures my mouth with a searing kiss.

He breaks away, and I'm breathless as he presses his forehead to mine, holding my hip, his other hand still over my thrashing heart. The heart—I fear—that may already belong to my brother.

The realization breaks me, and my eyes start to water as I look at him. His brows furrow, and he tilts his head questioningly as a tear slips down my cheek.

"I can't marry you," I whisper. "Mom is going to make me marry some asshole, and I won't ever be able to have you."

Is that the wrong thing to say to him? He most likely isn't feeling the same way. He's not capable of those emotions—but

I need to be honest with myself, even once, that this could be, or is, more than just me teaching him how to be sexual with someone.

He admitted he felt different, something he couldn't control. So there's a chance he cares about me past being his teacher-sister.

Stupid feelings. Why can't I have feelings for Adam? Why Malachi? Why my brother?

Wordlessly, he slides his hand from my heart, up my chest, and wraps his fingers around my throat before slamming his mouth down on mine.

The kiss is brutal and hard and firm, his hand finding its way back under my skirt so he can skim his fingers over the wet spot of my panties.

"I'll ask Olivia if she wants to come," Dad says, but I'm too drawn into the moment to care what they're talking about as Malachi slides the fabric aside and drives two fingers home, making me huff a violent breath into his mouth. "Where is she?"

"I think she's in the main closet getting a pair of her shoes."

Just as the heat starts to build, the heavy footfalls of my father reach my ears, and I gasp and push my brother away from me, fixing my panties back into place as I hurry out of the closet, closing it with Malachi still inside. "Hey!" I say, far too excitedly, considering his son just had me pinned to the wall and was kissing me with his fingers in my pussy. My thighs are still trembling, soaked, with my need for release. I think my eyes are crossing, and they're definitely red.

We've been doing these lessons for months, but Malachi was a natural at kissing and using his fingers from the start.

Typical for Malachi Vize to be an overachiever, even when it comes to fucking around with his little sister and making her whimper his name and praise him while eating her out.

Dad's fixing his tie while saying, "There's an open day at the firm next week. I was going to ask if you wanted to come with your brother."

Oh, those words.

Yes, I would love to come with my brother. Maybe he'll take me somewhere on his motorbike and eat me out on it. Or better, bend me over it?

No—sick. Sick, sick, sick.

Dammit.

"Sure," I reply. "I'll make sure I don't have practice."

"Great, angel. You've always been a good girl. Hurry along before your mother gets bored and burns the house down while trying to bake another cake."

As much as she loves to cook, she can't bake to save herself.

I run down the stairs, swearing to myself since I left the shoes I was going to wear behind. I settle for the ones I have on and grab my purse, about to leave just as Malachi walks into the main lobby, his eyes on me as he licks his bottom lip.

"Did you clean out your tarantula's bed?" I ask as a cover.

He nods, and I shiver. I still hate spiders—I run out of his room whenever he decides to play with the fluffy monster.

Who even plays with a damn spider and finds it fun?

He's insane.

Mom leaves first, and Malachi's chest is still rising and falling harshly, his hungry eyes raking down my cheer uniform as he grabs my wrist before I can go after our mother. *Come to my room when you get home later.*

My smile is blinding, and I bite my lip like my high-school crush is flirting with me. I glance around to make sure no one can see and lift to my tiptoes, giving him a chaste kiss. "We'll move on to our next lesson," I whisper. "And I want to hear your voice while I'm bouncing all over your cock, big brother."

His nostrils flare, and I step back, certain his dick is already getting hard as I skip out of the manor, giggling when I hear my phone vibrate with a text I know is from him.

Malachi: *Since you're teaching me everything else, will you teach me how to say your name? I might fuck the pronunciation up a few times, but I want to know how to say it.*

I expected something dirty from him, but my brows furrow as I reread the message, my heart racing in my chest. The warmth it sends through me has me fighting a grin, a blush all over my face. He hasn't spoken a word once since coming to live with us—but he *wants* to say my name. What does that mean?

I reply with a "Sure," and close off my screen as Mom turns on the radio of her SUV and heads to the mall.

After Mom drags me through far too many stores and has me carrying all her bags, she drops me at Abigail's house. We cheer together—we have since we were thirteen. She's the funny one between us. The one who sees the light in every bad situation. She's also quite short compared to me, and has purple, bobbed hair to match her personality. We're kind of opposites, but maybe that's why we're best friends?

She's forever complaining that her hair never grows to the length of my brown curls but then she goes and bleaches it every other week, so what does she expect?

She walks out of her front door, huffing and giving her father the middle finger when the door slams shut. "Asshole," she mutters. "Are you still staying over tonight?"

"Sure," I reply, even though I want to say no. That I changed my mind. I want Malachi to sneak in through my window, to wake me up, or maybe not wake me up, while he buries his face between my legs.

Thoughts of waking up in the middle of that scene has created the perfect vision in my head—something I'm going to bring up with Malachi. Maybe he'll be into it, maybe not, but I want him to be the one to live the fantasy with me.

I'm not sure if it means anything, but I've always liked it rough. Abbi thinks I'm a BDSM whore, but I'm not. I don't like gags and whips, but the idea of being chased? Degraded? Taken against my will?

I like the thought of being fucked savagely. To run from them—him. To be terrified while orgasming. I want to be choked until my vision blurs while Malachi fucks me with his fingers—while he forces his cock in either hole and makes me bleed and cry and scream for God.

Is there something wrong with me?

Maybe it's the family I came from—exposing me to a vile life at such a young age before I was rescued. But surely something like that couldn't cause me to have such fantasies, right?

Should I ask my brother if he feels the same, since we have similar backgrounds?

No. I think Malachi would be mortified if I ever told him the things going on in my head—it felt bad enough putting his hand to my throat, even if the way he robbed me of air made me even wetter. But then again, he aims to please, and having him destroy me sexually would more than please me.

The hour of practice drags. I want to go home and lie in bed—watch a movie and eat junk food—not get drunk around loads of college kids. We try numerous pyramid stances with me as the flyer, where I'm thrown forward to flip onto my back. Anna nearly drops me, and she apologizes over and over—but I pat her shoulder. "It's fine. Just be more focused."

Her cheeks heat.

Anna, the blonde Malachi went on a date with months ago. Well, I wouldn't say a date, since he freaked out and left, but still… he agreed to the date. Does that mean he's attracted to her? Does he still talk to her?

Anna is beautiful—and to add to my list of things to be jealous about, she's also a lovely person. The best of both worlds—someone with a great soul who looks like she was born to be a supermodel.

She's slim and tanned. Smart. She was also prom queen, so it makes no sense for her to want to go out with Malachi, considering he's still seen as a freak. The weird kid who never had friends until he left school—the smoker who drives around on a motorbike and needs his sister to show him how to kiss.

We finish up and go into the locker room to shower and change—I head to my locker at the back of the room, away from everyone, then I grab my things and set them on the bench, brushing my hair while they all talk opposite the locker.

"Are you coming to Abbi's party tonight?" I hear one of the girls ask. "I heard she invited loads of guys."

"I have my eyes on someone," someone else replies. "Do you think Malachi Vize will be there?"

"The hot mute guy? Looks like he wants to murder everyone while giving off big dick energy?"

I pause as I go through my gym bag, eavesdropping like I'm listening to gossip. Even as my heart rate picks up its pace, I focus on their muffled words.

"Yeah, him. He was the one Anna was in the room with a few months back. I think she gave him head or something."

"Really? I thought they fucked?"

I frown and drop my shirt, curling my hair over my ear as if it'll help my hearing.

"Did Anna say that? Maybe they did. Hey, do you think he moans? Or would it just be like… breathy? Should we ask her if the rumors are true, and he has his cock pierced?"

I grit my teeth and shove the rest of my things into my bag, my eyes already burning.

The door opens before I can make my presence felt, and more of the girls come in.

"Oh, Anna! I have a question about the mute. Did you fuck him a few months ago at the party? And if so, does he moan?"

"Shhhhh! Olivia is his sister," Anna hisses. "I don't want things to be weird on the team if she finds out I'm screwing her brother."

"So you're *still* screwing him? Give us details! Is he big? Dominant? Does he carve a satanic mark into your body with sheep's blood while he fucks you?"

"Damn, Danara, calm down."

"I'm asking what y'all are thinking."

I've had enough—I finish stuffing my things into my bag, tie my hair back, storm from the lockers and shoulder past the girls—Danara especially. I ignore them as I march out of the locker room, burning tears starting to slide down my cheeks.

The betrayal hurts.

I hear someone call my name but fuck them. Fuck all of them for talking about my brother like he's some weirdo. And fuck my brother for lying to me.

He snuck into my room and asked me to teach him because he freaked out on his date with Anna, but all along, he'd fucked her? Was still fucking her?

Is that why he was such a natural in everything he was doing to me?

While I storm to the bus station, refusing to drive with Abbi, I pull out my phone, my fingers shaking as they type his name to bring up his contact details. I never call—it makes no sense to call since he doesn't talk. He probably won't answer. But he doesn't need to say a word—the asshole just needs to listen.

Three rings then silence, the call connecting without that usual greeting. I don't mean to cry, but tears drench my cheeks as little puffs of air escape from my lungs, audible enough he'll know I'm upset.

"How dare you, Malachi. How fucking *dare* you? You lied

to me. You… Y-You lied. You lied and tricked me into teaching you everything, you goddamn *freak*. I thought I was helping you, and I was falling for you in the process, yet all along you knew damn well what to fucking do! What sort of sicko does that? I'm your sister! And I… I was…"

I cover my mouth with the back of my hand and crouch in the parking lot, sobbing into my hand. "I hope screwing Anna was worth ruining whatever fucked-up relationship we had. You'll never get near me again, Malachi." I shake my head, my jaw jittering. "Never. I hate you. I h-h-hate you so fucking much."

I can hear him breathing heavily on the other end, a message coming through.

Malachi: *Where are you?*

"Fuck you," I spit before hanging up.

CHAPTER 9
OLIVIA

"**A**re you sure you're okay, angel?"

I sigh, walking up the grand staircase. "Yeah. Just a rough day. I didn't mean to worry you." I'd called him as soon as I hung up on Malachi, in tears, my heart breaking, but when he answered, I froze, not knowing what to say.

I don't want my dad to be disappointed in me, and as much as I despise Malachi, I don't want him getting into trouble for manipulating his little sister into doing sexual acts with him.

I sniffle, and he huffs. "You're lying to me, but we'll talk when I'm home."

"Okay," I whisper. "I love you, Dad."

"I love you too, angel. Go get some rest. I'll bring home some takeout for you and your brother."

My jaw rolls, and I plaster a fake smile on my face. "Thank you."

He hangs up, and I close my eyes, standing at my door and pressing my forehead to the wood. My heart is sore—is that a thing? I feel like I've been cheated on by a long-term boyfriend, or someone punched me right in the gut and ripped my heart out.

When I get into my room, the curtains are drawn. Malachi is sitting on my bed with his back to me, his hood up, flicking his lighter, so my dark room glows.

I freeze in the doorway, standing aside. "Get out," I grit. "I don't want to even look at you."

He turns to face me, but I avert my gaze, refusing to look him in the eye. "Leave, Malachi." A huff, and I slouch against the door, exhausted from crying. "Whatever we were doing is over. I want you to leave my room, and don't ever come near me again."

He's signing, but I'm not looking at him.

His motorbike boots quickly come towards me, a grip on my chin forcing me to look up at him, but I keep my eyes to the side. I don't want to see his face or learn what bullshit excuse he's going to come out with. I want him gone from my life—or at least from my fucking room.

"Can you please leave?" I ask, my voice breaking, cracking in two like my heart. "You hurt me, and I can't look at you."

He cups my face between his hands, pressing his forehead to mine, breathing heavily, but I pull back when he tries to kiss me, my hand moving before I can think and slapping him across the face. "Get the fuck out!"

He tries to communicate with his hands again, but I stop him, grabbing his fingers to halt whatever he's going to say. It's the worst, most belittling way to treat him, to silence his only way of talking, but I don't care. He hurt me, and I don't want to hear his side.

I shove him in the chest and walk to my vanity, grabbing the largest perfume bottle there and throwing it at him, hitting his shoulder. "Leave!"

He shakes his head and comes for me, signing, *Let me fucking explain.*

"Fuck you," I seethe, slapping him across the face again when he gets close enough, his cheek red. "I hate you; do you understand that, you fucking freak? I hate you for tricking me. For manipulating me into doing things for you."

Malachi tries to sign again, but I grip his fingers, twisting them, making him grit his teeth with discomfort, but he doesn't stop me. It's like he's enjoying the pain, the way I'm hitting him, the voice I'm using as I scream at him.

And that dark little voice in my head enjoys it too.

I shove at his chest again and again and again, until he snatches my wrists and pushes me into the wall. His mouth opens, as if he's trying to say something, his lips shaping, no sound coming from them until he's whispering, "Ol... Ol...

N-N…"

I shake my head and duck under his arm, grabbing the door handle. "Go," I say sternly. "Just… just go, Malachi. There's nothing to resolve here."

We were going to be each other's firsts, he signs, his eyes searching my face erratically. *We were—*

I turn away from him and laugh, leaving my bedroom and speed-walking down the hall, shaking my head. "I'm not a fucking virgin, Malachi. I haven't been since I was sixteen!" I spin around to face him again to see his defeated hands by his sides. "And apparently neither are you!"

I'm not a liar, he signs. *Believe me.*

"I'll never believe you again."

I turn away from him, but he grabs my hair and spins me back, slamming his mouth down on mine. I slap at his chest to push him away, but I'm pinned against the wall as his tongue pries between my lips, his arm around the small of my back as he tries to kiss me.

My nails drag down his cheek, and he hisses into my mouth.

I try to knee him, but he grabs my leg and hikes it to his hip, and I'm not sure when my hands start raking through his hair, or when I start kissing him back, but it's mind-numbing, and I can't stop the hum I release.

Malachi traps me under his devious spell as he devours my mouth, probably knowing it's the last time I'll ever let him kiss me. It feels different. I'm not the only person he's kissed, and he lied. He lied, and he tricked me, and I should hate him.

I shouldn't grind against him, feeling the pleasure rush through me, or enjoy the way his tongue darts forcefully against my own.

He nips and sucks on my tongue, tightening his hold around the small of my back while his hand palms my ass.

Little puffs of air gasp into my mouth as I sink my teeth into his lip—hard—making sure to hurt him. "I hate you," I pant, easing back to look him in the eyes. He watches a tear slide down my cheek, catching it with his tongue before dipping his head to my throat, sucking against my pulse and making me moan.

My hand drops between us, under his waistband, and I wrap my fingers around his cock, feeling the piercings running up the underside. I stroke him while he marks my neck, his grip on my ass growing painful as he thrusts into my hand.

His precum is leaking all over my hand, and I shove at his chest enough to drop to my knees, pulling down his biker combats as I go. His cock springs free, hard and long and thick, right in front of me.

Looking up at Malachi, I grip the base. "I hope when you see others on their knees for you, you see me, your innocent baby sister, with your cock in her mouth. I hope when I'm out of your life, you miss this sight, because as soon as you finish down my throat and I swallow all your big brotherly cum, you're going to pack all your shit and leave."

He swallows, his palm pressing to the wall above my head. "Do you understand?" I push, digging my nails into his cock, making him flinch and grow harder.

Nodding, he fists my hair with both hands and thrusts into my mouth, gagging me as the piercings slide against my tongue, the hoop at the tip hitting the back of my throat.

I lap up his precum, swirling my tongue around the tip as he rests his forehead on the wall, panting, sweating, his grip on my hair near unbearable.

I gasp for air after a few minutes of him hammering my throat, and when he swells more, he pulls out, drool connecting my lips to his cock. He looks down at me, fury in his eyes, and spits in my face.

"What the f—"

The next thing I know, Malachi pushes me onto my back, lying on top of me, forcing his tongue into my mouth while thrusting his hardness against my jeans.

He groans inaudibly and reaches down, unbuttoning them and yanking them harshly down. He hauls them off my legs and tosses them behind him, making them fly down the grand staircase we're at the top of.

Leaning over my half-naked body, he signs, *Tell me you're in love with me, little sister.*

"No," I grit.

He punches the ground next to my head, and my body seizes. *Say you love me. Say you feel the fucking same way I do about you!*

I tip my chin up. "I don't love you, Malachi. I could never love someone like you."

His jaw tenses. *Because I can't talk? Because I can't tell you how fucking breathtaking you are every second of every day? Because I can't breathe without being near you? Someone like me… I'm different—I can't be normal for you. I can't defend you without using my fists or my bat, and I can't touch you at the same time as telling you that you're everything to me. I can't whisper sweet nothings into your mouth and I can't fucking marry you because not only am I your brother, but I'm defective.*

He pushes up to his knees, his hands going nuts as he signs quickly, his eyes red with a mixture of heartbreak and rage I have no idea how to contain for him.

Believe me or don't, but you're the only person in my life, and you always have been. And when you take your last breath, or I take mine, that won't fucking change. You. Are. Mine. My goddamn property, do you understand?

A beat passes. Another. And another, and I gulp as I whimper out a soft sob. "You can't even feel love, so everything you're saying is another lie." I cover my face as my body wracks with each cry, my heart broken for the brother I can never have.

I don't look at him, so I can't see what he's signing, then he's tapping my arms to make me look, but I refuse and cry some more.

Until that cry turns into a moan, and Malachi has his mouth over the mound of my pussy, slipping his tongue through my entrance. I still don't move my hands from my face, even as I chase his mouth when he pulls back, flinching as he spits on my clit and sucks on the tender flesh of my folds. He parts my lips with his fingers, and thrusts his face between my legs, cutting off his oxygen.

My back bows, and I cry out, leaking my juices all over his tongue as he fucks me with it, his hand pushing my legs apart to open me more for him.

"Oh God," I moan, shivering as an orgasm already builds. "You're going to make me come, Malachi. Fuck. Fuck, fuck, fuck," I whimper, trying to grind my hips up, but he's holding me in place, capturing my clit between his teeth and spitting, sucking, my eyes pinging open as he sink a finger into my ass at the same time as thrusting two fingers into my pussy.

I tense everywhere as he pulls his fingers free and grips my thighs as his tongue fucks into my entrance, lapping up all my juices as my inner walls flutter.

"Angel?"

My dad's voice comes from the bottom of the stairs, and I somehow manage to perch on my elbows while Malachi bruises my thighs with his grip, sweat coating my skin as my dad stands with my discarded jeans in his hand, mortification all over his face.

"Daddy?" I whisper, my eyes rolling, falling back as my spine tingles, my breasts turning tender as my brother keeps eating me out, despite my dad being present.

He rushes up the stairs, stopping when he sees who's destroying his baby girl's pussy. "Malachi!"

Dad grabs his shoulder and tries to pull him away from me, but my brother's grip doesn't falter; nor do the strokes of his tongue, and we're both dragged across the floor while Dad tries to get him off me.

My brother doesn't stop, and my eyes close as my dad tries again. His mouth disconnects from my pussy, and I whimper from the loss, and the next thing, Malachi is being dragged off me, and Dad punches him.

Malachi's nose is bleeding when he stands up, gathering something in his mouth before he grabs Dad's jaw and spits in his face. *Your daughter tastes fucking delicious*, he signs. *Too bad she's all mine.*

Realization hits, and Dad grimaces and wipes at his face. "You disgusting piece of shit!" He launches himself at Malachi, who's grinning as he drives his fist into our father's face over and over again.

I bend my knees to hide myself, backing up against the wall as he grabs the lapels of my father's suit jacket and slams his head into his face so harshly, Dad falls back.

"She's your goddamn sister!" Dad bellows as he tries to get up, smearing blood on his face, and Malachi silently laughs, wiping the back of his hand across his mouth, spreading the blood dripping from his nose, then kicking him in the face.

"Stop," I bark. "Don't you dare hit him again."

His eyes snap to me, and I shrink on the spot.

But then he fists his hands, his jaw tensing as if liquid rage has been injected into his veins. He grabs Dad by the hair and knees him in the face, knocking him back, then climbs on him, landing fist after fist, punch after punch, on his face.

"Stop!" I scream, trying to pull Malachi off him, but he shrugs me away and drags our dad to the stairs before picking him up and kicking him down every single step.

He smacks his head on the way, and as I try to run down to him, Malachi grabs me by the hair at the back of my head, forcing me to trail down after him instead. I slap at his arms, scratching him, yelling at him to let me go, but when we get to the bottom of the staircase, my dad lies limp on the floor, blood leaking from his head.

"No!" I run at him, and Malachi lets me. I cup Dad's cheeks between my hands, blood soaking his face. "Daddy? Daddy, can you hear me?"

A presence behind me makes me freeze, and I glance over my shoulder to see Malachi getting on his knees behind me, stroking his cock from the base, up over all his piercings, twisting at the tip. His bottom lip is captured between his teeth, and I gasp as he shoves my shirt up and over my ass.

I try to sit up, but he snatches my nape and keeps me on all fours, pushing my head onto my dad's chest. His heart is beating so fast, like a drum, as Malachi lines the head of his cock up to my entrance.

He's not going to…

Against my inner turmoil, and the fear that my dad might be dying, my pussy aches for him. It's vile and wrong and sick, but I need him inside me.

He rubs his piercings against my core, spreading my arousal, his fingers digging deeper into my nape as he eases the head in, inch by inch, and my breath hitches from the thickness, the way my body can't accommodate his size, his girth nearly splitting me open as he sinks in to the hilt.

His breaths are stilted, and I bet if he used his voice, they'd be deep, pleasurable moans as he eases out, fucking back in like a hammer on a nail. I'm struggling to breathe with how intense it feels. Warm liquid gathers around my knees, and I know it's my dad's blood.

My body lunges forward each time Malachi thrusts into me, and I feel so dirty for enjoying it. I'm enjoying my brother fucking me on top of my father's limp body. His heart is beating, but blood is still puddling around me, and I yelp as Malachi slaps my ass and goes harder, faster, jerking me and my dad on the floor as he wraps my hair around his fist and uses it to drag my head back.

Hips snapping into mine, he pants, holding my hip as his thrusts become even more powerful. The metal lining his cock rubs on my sweet spot, and my eyes roll, my nerve endings sizzling as I whimper.

"Harder," I moan, ashamed that I'm loving the feel of his cock filling me up. "Go harder, Malachi."

He does. Each punch of his hips has my lungs threatening to catch fire, and the pain on my scalp from him tugging my hair has my spine twisting so pleasantly, I see stars forming in my vision.

My brother bends forward, plastering his front to my back, and tilts my head so he can kiss me. It's brutal, bruising, and he fucks into me as he swallows my moans, my gasps for him to go faster, deeper, to make me come all over his cock.

He breathes heavily into my mouth as he slows his movements, going deep and dragging the metal against that spot that has me tensing everywhere.

"Are you going to make me come on my big brother's cock?" I whisper.

He nods, mouth open as he inaudibly groans and lets go of my hair, sliding his hand up my ribs, between my breasts, so he can squeeze my throat.

My words are cut off, along with my air, and my eyes feel

the pressure as Malachi grinds into me. My inner walls clutch around his dick, and the pleasurable heat shoots from my curling toes, all the way to my core, as I silently scream and come all over his cock.

I clench around his thickness repeatedly, my back arching, and he stills, finding his own release as he fills me with each drop of his forbidden cum.

He only stays in place for a second before pulling out and shoving himself away from me. He's standing as I push up onto my palms, seeing all the blood I hadn't realized had soaked into my face and hands and chest.

My hands shake, though nowhere near as much as my legs do as I sit up on my haunches, and I glance over at Malachi as he tucks his cock away, wiping his face, his chest rising and falling. I stare at my father's body, bleeding and twitching, my wide eyes lifting to Malachi again. He doesn't seem to care as I reach down to check my dad's pulse, which is weak but present.

"Dad, stay with me. I'm going to get you to hospital," I say with a shaky voice as I pull on my panties and jeans, Malachi's cum already leaking out of me.

I shoulder past Malachi and run to the kitchen, slamming my fist on the emergency button on the wall, sending signals to the nearest cop car and ambulance.

I glance up at Malachi as he follows me back to my father's

body. "I'll give you a head start," I snarl, trembling, the sirens already sounding nearby. "Run, Malachi."

PART TWO

MALACHI

8 YEARS LATER

CHAPTER 10
MALACHI

My beautiful Olivia.

My beautiful, smart, and twisted Olivia. You may have everyone else fooled with your kindness, with your warm smiles and soft voice, using them to get what you want in life—but I know you. I know the real you. Not this fake façade you show to those near you—your posture, your style of clothes, the way you let those delicate moans slip free when you ride your own hand, thinking of what we could've had if you hadn't testified against me.

I know the depths of your depravity and the way your mind works. I know you more than you know yourself, you little fucking minx.

My foster sister's touch is like a tattoo on my skin even now, all these years later. The way she whimpered my name against my lips, how tightly her cunt gripped my cock when I fucked her over our dying father's body, coated in his blood.

I'm just biding my time. Waiting in the shadows and watching her receive all the gifts I leave her. They make her nervous. She hates chocolates and flowers and jewelry, so I shower her with them. She's on edge, yet I think she likes to be scared. No—I know she likes the thrill of fear. Her journal goes into great detail about her dark desires; how much she yearns to be stalked, chased, kidnapped, and taken.

So, being the ever-loving big brother that I am, I intend to bring all her fucked-up fantasies to life while she begs for my forgiveness.

She's been waiting for me—the brother who was released from prison six months ago. She looks for me and searches my name on the internet five times a day, trying to find where I am, messaging her friends that if I was going to come for her, I would've already done so.

I still have the voicemails she left on my phone. Drunken ones. Sad ones. Angry ones. I've listened to all of them, saved them on my computer so I can hear her crying that she hates me yet misses me, that she's sorry for the way everything went when we were teenagers.

Sorry. Sorry, sorry, sorry.

Fucking sorry.

That damn word echoes in my psyche—a curse that won't fuck off.

Sorry's just a word to try to get out of something, to dodge trouble if you've been caught out. Sorry's a five-letter disgrace that shouldn't even need to be used. It should be abolished from the fucking dictionary. Actions do speak louder than words, and if she's as sorry as she makes out in her voicemails, then why does she sometimes look happy? Why is she going out partying with her friends? Kissing guys who—shockingly—vanish days later?

Why does she dance around her apartment, singing ridiculous songs about love?

Why is she living her life without me?

If the bitch is sorry, then why is she only looking me up on the internet and not hunting for me? Why isn't she looking for me?

It fucking irks me that she didn't visit me, not once. I refused any and all visitation from others, but I asked her to come and see me. I wrote to her the first two years, waiting patiently for a written reply, a presence, a smile to my fucking face that never came.

She left me in there to rot.

Well, little sister, no need to look for me anymore. I'm right here, and I intend to stick around until I've broken you.

I'll break her the way she broke me. I'm going to make her terrified, make her scream for help while I fuck her tight ass and force her to *show* she's sorry.

For those eight years, I didn't communicate with a single

soul. I've kept my voice to myself, where no one else can take it, since I was five years old. The one time I tried to use it, I struggled to pronounce her name, and Olivia yelled at me that I was a liar, that she hated me, that we were done, and slapped me across the face before I could get her name past my lips.

I've been stuck in my own purgatory since I was born—the different one, the black sheep, the fucking mute weirdo who has an intense fascination with his little sister.

I mean, who wouldn't find her fascinating?

Staying behind her—not too far, but close enough that I can see the peachy outline of her ass in that tight, cock-hardening dress—I shove my hands in my pockets and keep my eyes on her.

Her porcelain skin glows in the sun while she walks with her face in her phone, ignoring the outside world like there aren't hundreds of people walking past her.

It's the same routine every morning. Me following behind undetected. Her with those ridiculously high heels, turning left and entering the small coffee shop for her usual morning coffee. While I smoke a cigarette across the road, she'll order, check the magazines for anything new, and then she'll smile at the barista. The same barista I've imagined diced and in small bags in my chest freezer.

The only reason the person isn't dead is that my sister's smile will drop as soon as she leaves, and then she'll take another left to the courthouse. It's not far from where we live. A short walk that brings me joy from being on the same trail as her as I listen to her heels clicking on the sidewalk. With my hood up and my cap hiding most of my face, my head down, she never notices me walking her to work.

My sister works with our mother. An assistant. A fucking hot piece of ass that all the dickheads want whenever she walks in. They don't care that she's engaged—to my own fucking dismay—yet I'm shocked it took this long for Mom to nail her down to someone. Adam turned out to be gay, Parker still can't walk properly, and all the other suitors she's had over the past six months have mysteriously vanished from existence.

You're fucking welcome, Olivia.

They weren't enough for you. No one is except me.

The guy she's supposed to marry is some businessman who made a deal with our parents. They'd invest together, build an empire, but only if Olivia Vize married their son, Xander.

She's hasn't even met the fucker. Mom seems to be giving her some time before the wedding is booked. A wedding I'll blow the fuck up if it goes ahead. I'll make sure I kill my dad this time, and I'll strangle Mom with his intestines and force Olivia to marry me instead, then I'll cage the bitch and feed her my cock when she's hungry.

Once she disappears into the building, I set off to her apartment like I do every day. It's the same routine, the same journey. I'll wake in my flat—coincidentally across from hers—and I'll watch the cameras as she gets washed, dressed, has some breakfast, then I'll grab my coat when she leaves the house.

We spend a lot of time together, me and my sister; she just doesn't know about it.

My favorite time is when she drinks the spiked alcohol in her fridge. I get to come over and care for her. Sometimes, I'll wash her hair and cuddle her in bed, and other times, I watch her stumble around her apartment, in the dark, thinking my shadow is part of her nightmares.

The fucking control I always need when she starts stripping her clothes off while drugged up… I deserve a goddamn medal for not shoving my cock in her cunt or mouth.

I crack open her door and deeply inhale, enjoying her scent, which is all over the apartment. It's the only time I get to smell her, apart from when I'm fumbling around with her unconscious form.

My apartment is on the same level as hers, but across the street. I was kind of shocked she wasn't living it up in some mansion like we were raised in, as if she wants some normality before she's launched into the life of the rich asshole she's tied to. I still need to deal with him, but the heavy protection he has is a bit of a ball-ache.

I check all the cameras are still hidden, pour myself a coffee—the same way she makes hers—and sit down on her sofa. Kicking my feet up, I sigh and look at the pictures littering her wall.

Her graduating college, though she doesn't use her qualification. Her with a dog that died a year ago. Her and a boyfriend she had while I was locked up for eight years—her fucking doing by the way. Some pictures with friends.

And my favorite, the largest on the wall, one of the two of us. Her kissing my cheek when we were sixteen and seventeen, when I was in a state of confusion over why I hit a boner every time I looked at my sister.

She has a necklace over the frame. There's a smaller image of us in that too. Younger. Me on her back at the beach. I'm a slim dickhead in it—no ink, no muscles—and I'm wearing a blue shirt that says something about fucking sharks.

Mom knew I hated sharks, but she bought me it anyway.

Fuck her too. I drew a mustache on her picture, but Olivia has yet to notice.

Fuck that entire family.

Except the daughter. She's hot and kind of imprinted on my brain.

My dear, sweet, innocent sister. I still see her distraught face while I sat before her in handcuffs, the way she couldn't look at me while she testified against me, ultimately sending me to prison for attempted murder on her precious daddy.

Dad ended up with brain damage—loss of memory and use

of some body parts. So she got away without losing her Vize status, since our dad has no recollection of why the fight broke out.

He interrupted my meal—maybe now he'll know better than to take away my food, the fucking asshole.

He should've died. I wanted him to die. I still do. He takes up so much of Olivia's attention—she's always wheeling him around in his chair, opening his food for him, feeding him. She kisses his cheek every time she leaves the manor. I know this because I have cameras set up there too. I have cameras everywhere she goes.

My girl never needs to worry about anyone hurting her, because her wonderful, ex-con, apparently psychotic brother is free and keeping her out of harm's way.

It's a pity I can't protect her from myself. Her betrayal isn't something I can shrug off like everything else. Her fucking people while I was locked away, having relationships, being happy, was unacceptable, but I let it all slide after squashing each element. But earning my forgiveness won't be easy—I'll have the whore begging on her knees for me to forgive her for all her fucking sins against me.

Her laptop dings, and I drop my feet and walk over to her small desk. The screen brightens, and I watch the messages fly back and forth between her and her friends in a group chat. They're discussing Halloween this weekend, a festival they want to go to. One of her friends, Anna, the one who caused this entire colossal fuck-up, says she's not going to a party while pregnant with twins, and another asked if they're too old to party.

Not gonna lie, Anna is lucky I care about her friend and her opinion of me, because I fully intended to strangle her when I got out. I even went to her address in the middle of the night and made a plan for where I'd stash her body—but, of course, she had to go and get pregnant, didn't she? Olivia would never forgive me if I killed her. I'm mad at my sister, but I don't want to give her any more reasons to hate me.

It's not a fair game yet.

Olivia gives her the middle-finger emoji, and I chuckle while sipping my coffee in her This Princess Loves Hugs mug.

Abigail: We're 26, you asshole! Just because you settled down doesn't mean we need to. Stop being a party pooper and get a costume picked.

Olivia: I already have my costume. Did you get the Poison Ivy outfit?

Abigail: Yes! I can't wait to see yours. Are you still going as a goth bride as a fuck you to your parents?

*Olivia: *Wink emoji* I'm very mature.*

I straighten, glancing over at her bedroom. It's tidy. The entire fucking house is tidy, the little clean freak that she is. I kind of love watching her putting music on and dancing around in her panties while she vacuums. One of my favorite pastimes with my cock in my hand.

I pull open her wardrobe and spot the costume that wasn't there yesterday, and my dick hardens at the thought, the fucking image in my head of her dressed up as a bride in black—the black tutu and corset, black netted tights and garter… I rub the material of the veil, gulping at the possibility of losing her to some other asshole when she marries.

I slam the wardrobe door harder than necessary, fist my hands, and screw my eyes shut. *Breathe, Malachi. Fucking breathe and don't wreck the place.*

Focus. Repress.

I open my eyes and shake it off.

If my girl is going out for Halloween, it looks like I am too. I can't wait to reacquaint my cock with her cunt—that one time with her over Dad's prone body replays in my mind, but it's not enough.

After reading in her journal that she would love to be taken while unconscious, I've been tempted to fuck her in her drugged-up state, to ram my cock in her ass too, but I want her eyes on me—I want her lucid, watching me fucking take what she took away from me.

I want to hear her screaming in both fear and pleasure while she reacquaints her throat with my cock and cries for mercy.

I won't show her any. That little shit took eight years from me. And this weekend, while she dresses up as a slutty bride, I'm going to make her pay.

Once I eat one of her apples and toss aside the core, I intentionally kick over her laundry basket and leave the toilet seat up, then place the chocolates on her table. I look around her place once more before I leave, then pull on my motorbike helmet and fix my gloves onto my hands as I make my way across the street to my bike.

The closest costume store isn't too far away, and I can't help but feel excitement—she likes to be scared while turned on, and she's going to be fucking terrified while I chase her down and choke the life out of her.

CHAPTER 11
MALACHI

The costume store smells funky.

Skulls everywhere. Hockey masks. Some blank faces. I contemplate the black one with the spider effect, but I want something more. The Jason mask looks like it's covered in years-old dust, and I squint at the corner of the store, where there's a row of three other masks.

Heavy boots take me there, the light above me flickering like I'm some sort of bad entity haunting the place.

My gaze falls on a black gas mask—two chambers on each side, rusty looking, the eyes covered in mesh. My lip curls at the corner, and I reach for it, feeling the weight of it in my hands, the rough texture of the design, imagining wearing it, my darling Olivia having no idea it's me behind the mask while she sucks my cock.

Nothing else here calls to me, so I pay for it and head back to my apartment. After I shower and cook some dinner, I sit at my desk. Screens litter the wall in front of me, showing everywhere Olivia goes, and I search each one to find her.

She's standing in her friend's kitchen, sipping from a mug and laughing at something Anna's husband is saying. Her friend rubs her pregnant belly, and Olivia presses her hand to it, her eyes widening. I see no reason to be happy here. Why is she smiling like that?

Babies are just reincarnations of the devil in my opinion, so I have no desire to ever become a father. I'd be terrible anyway. I wouldn't ever want a miniature version of me stealing my attention from my sister. I'm an asshole—why would I want another one of me?

When I filled Olivia up with my cum, I loved the way it dripped out of her cunt. I wanted to spread it over her pussy and shove it back inside, not wanting to waste a drop. But I never wanted to get her pregnant—that would've been a fucking disaster.

The first year of my imprisonment, I thought Olivia's silence was because she was pregnant—that I'd got her pregnant from that one time, and I even started asking her in letters if the kid was mine, tricking myself into believing I had a kid out there that was taking all of her attention from me.

She wasn't visiting me because she had a bastard chained to her.

Thankfully, she's still childless and on birth control, so no pregnancies or babies or shitty diapers. Fuck, wait—what if her future husband wants to knock her up?

I sit forward and open up my search bar, hunting to see if there's any way to perform a hysterectomy safely at home, but I fail to find a single article. I huff and lean my elbow on the desk, fist to my temple, and wonder if I can drug the guy and hire a doctor to snip him.

Less invasive than doing it to Olivia. It's a win-win. My girl doesn't want to be a mother anyway.

Olivia kisses her friend's cheek, waves to the little girl in the highchair, then goes to her car. I sigh and watch her drive off, and wait until she drops into another screen. Ten minutes later, she pulls into her usual gas station, pays for her gas and some chips, then gets back into her car.

By the time she gets home, it's dark out. My lights are off as I stand by the window, watching her struggle to find her key to the entrance of her building. She drops her phone and stamps her foot, which makes me smile as I take a draw of my cigarette.

The little things she does make me feel all warm and fuzzy, and I need to remind myself she's a snake with a pretty face and a tight pussy.

She vanishes into the building, and I turn to watch the screens again, keeping the smoke between my lips while I zoom in on all the cameras in her apartment. She drops her keys on the table beside the door, freezing in place when she sees the box of chocolates.

Her bag slips from her shoulder, and I grin as she walks towards it slowly, lifting the box and reading the little note I left.

You look so beautiful today, sweet Olivia.

As usual, she tosses the chocolates in the trash and crushes the note before throwing it aside. "Leave me alone!" she yells, kicking her bag in annoyance, stopping when she sees her laundry basket tipped over and her clothes on the ground. She rolls her eyes and checks her apples—always ten, but I eat one daily, just to annoy her more.

The toilet seat is up too, so she slaps it down and groans to herself. "Fucking weirdo," she mutters, and my smile slips at the use of the insult everyone used to throw at me.

She opens her wine bottle, fills the glass with the drug-filled liquid, and I wait patiently for her to pass out on the sofa before I turn off my screens and head over.

She's snoring lightly when I arrive, the wine spilled on the floor, staining her rug. I clean it up and wipe the drool from her mouth.

I run her a warm bath, add some oils, and wait until it bubbles up, using her fingerprint to unlock her phone and turn on the playlist she listens to while bathing.

She's limp in my arms as I lift her, and I pause for a moment when her head flops into my chest and her hair goes in my face. I inhale, closing my eyes and burying my head in her shoulder, feeling that warmth again and wondering if she'd allow this if she was conscious.

Doubt it. I'd be shocked if she didn't try to beat the shit out of me then call the cops for stalking and drugging her.

I press a kiss to her forehead and carry her to the bathroom, lowering us both to the floor while a Lana Del Rey song plays from her phone. I push the sleeves of her dress down her arms until the material is at her hips then unclip her bra, her perky breasts bouncing as I pull them free.

Ignoring the intense need to capture a nipple between my teeth is harder than my cock right now. I inwardly groan and yank the rest of her dress down her legs, pressing my forehead to her shins and breathing, trying to regain my composure before I sit up and hook my fingers into her panties.

I slide the fabric down her soft, smooth legs to reveal her pussy. Every single time I do this, I struggle not to touch her. She's perfection on the outside—beautiful, stunning, a work of fucking art that was born to drive me more insane than I already am.

My cock thickens even further, and I bite my lip, my thighs tensing. She's lying on the ground, out cold, naked, and I feel like I'm dying inside.

If Malachi was free, I'd want it to be him to make all my fantasies come true, she had written in her journal.

I spread her legs, closing my eyes again and counting to three, keeping my hand on her thigh. Without looking, I glide my palm up, letting out a shaky breath when I reach the apex of her thigh, my thumb on her mound. I dig my fingers into her skin, and my eyes ping open as she whimpers.

She's still drugged up and far from conscious, but her hips rock upwards a little, and she makes a soft noise when my thumb presses to her clit. Short puffs of air escape her lips as I rub the pad of my thumb over it, circling slowly, my mouth fucking watering as I bring myself closer.

She's enjoying this.

I should keep going.

I part her pussy with my other hand, opening her wide for me. My face dives between her legs and I inhale her scent, my dick fucking aching to be released from the confines of my pants.

I want to tell her how intoxicating her cunt is; that her glistening arousal on the tip of my nose is making me delusional, insanity running wild in my mind. If I could use my voice, I'd tell her how perfect she was, that I wish I could stay between her legs forever.

I won't talk. I can barely string a sentence together, even when I was training my voice box in my cell to produce four syllables without pausing.

Pathetic, in all honesty. Wanting to say Olivia's name and struggling to do so made me drive my fist into too many walls.

I know how to fucking talk. I do. But I just... can't without making a fool of myself. I stutter, and my tone is all over the place.

One or two words are fine. As long as they aren't a mouthful or tongue-twisters.

When the time comes, I will find it in me to tell her what I really think of her—how I *feel* when I look at her.

Olivia lifts her hips, trying to chase my mouth as I pull back. My girl wants me. She wants to be fucked while sleeping.

Her cunt is glistening from her arousal, and I ease my middle finger in, her tight walls clutching as I sink deeper then stop circling her clit and replace my thumb with my mouth.

I hum against her as I suck on her clit, and her hips move slightly again, rocking her pussy against my tongue and finger. I add a second finger, curling them inside her while I flick my tongue.

Delicious, exactly like I remember. I fuck her with my fingers, sucking, biting, grinding my cock against her motionless leg. She cries out softly as she soaks my hand with her arousal, and I stop when I hear the water pouring over the side of the tub.

Sighing, I pull my fingers out of her and get to my knees,

turning off the tap and releasing some of the water down the drain.

My anger knows no bounds, because I want to smash the tub up for interrupting us.

I unbuckle my belt and free my cock, fisting the base and giving it a stroke, watching the wetness on her thighs, her hole calling to my cock, begging me to come home.

My balls are heavy, needing a release, and I stroke myself again, my piercing sliding against my palm as I line up the head of my cock to her cunt, gasping as I push into her.

Fuck.

She's so damn tight—her pussy is gripping me like a fucking fist.

I'll make it fit, I think to myself, pushing in a little deeper.

Olivia has a string of drool down her chin. I wipe it away with my thumb and move the hair from her face as I pull out a few inches and thrust back in to the hilt.

Her brows knit together, and I press my forehead to hers, breathing her in as I fuck into her, my balls slapping against her thigh the faster I go.

So wet, so fucking mine, even when she's not aware of it.

I press my mouth to hers, slipping my tongue between her lips as I groan, pounding into her harder, faster, deeper, grabbing her leg and hiking it up to get a better angle than this missionary shit.

I can taste the wine on my tongue as I suck on hers, and I falter when I feel her kiss me back. Or try to. She's rocking against me lightly, nowhere near the way I'm hammering into her, breathing heavily while her eyes flutter.

"Malachiiii."

I pause, nearly releasing inside her from my name slurring from her mouth.

Her eyes are closed. I slap her cheek lightly, but she doesn't wake. Does that mean she's dreaming of me?

I draw back and pummel into her harder, making her inner walls crush my cock.

Fuck. I haven't had sex in eight years, nearly nine, and it all feels natural. The way I thrust, hitting her sweet spot with my piercings, dragging moans from her as I suck on her mouth. I drop my head and take one of her tightening nipples into my mouth, and she's arching completely off the floor, taking me deeper, letting out a strangled moan as she grows warmer, wetter, shaking beneath me.

She chokes on air as I sink my teeth into her nipple, biting hard, making sure it hurts, which only has her pussy clutching me repeatedly, her scream muffled as I fuck her into an orgasm.

It doesn't take me long to follow her. My balls tighten into my body, my legs tense up, and my spine goes stiff as I fill her with my cum, stilling my cock deep inside her clenching pussy.

I let her nipple pop from my mouth and kiss a harsh trail

up her chest and jaw to her lips as she falls back into a fully unconscious state.

I pull my cock out of her, rid myself of the rest of my clothes, and lift her into the tub with me. With her back to my front, I lie back, listening to the music with my eyes closed, heart still racing.

Well, this is relaxing. Usually I'm in this position and trying to fight the urge to touch her. But since that's already been covered, I can just... relax.

Olivia's skin has always been soft, a few freckles dusting her shoulders, and I kiss each one of them while I wash her, soaking her hair and reaching for her strawberry-scented shampoo. I love the way her hair feels between my fingers, the way the shampoo lathers in my hands as I clean it.

I use her sponge on her arms and legs, and she whimpers as I drop it between her thighs and wipe away the evidence of me fucking her. I kiss her throat, feeling her pulse beneath my lips, before wrapping my arms around her.

Once I get her dried and into a pair of her silky PJs, I tuck her into bed and kiss her forehead, pulling the covers up to her chin. I stroke her hair, rubbing it between my fingers. It's a bit wet—I could only dry so much of it with the towel before I got fed up.

I clean the tub with a cloth, mop up our cum and the water from the floor, and make sure the small mat is exactly where it was before I fucked her on it. Hands to my hips, I tilt my head and look at the fluffy thing. Was it straighter? Will she realize it's been moved?

Huffing, I turn off the light and head to the kitchen, pausing when I see all the dishes in the sink. My eyes roll before I rinse them off then fill her dishwasher and turn it on. I fix her apple stack, straighten out her mugs, then chew my lip as I glance around for anything else I might have messed with prior to her being drugged.

I already cleaned up the wine, but there's still a little stain on her carpet, so I get on my hands and knees and scrub at it until it's unidentifiable.

I empty the filter in her coffee machine, then empty her trashcan and tie the bag, leaving it by the door for me to take when I leave.

Really, where would she be without me?

Olivia is still asleep when I get back to her room, and I yawn and drop onto the bed beside her, exhausted from tidying up after fucking her.

I grab her phone, unlock it with her finger, and swipe through her photos. There's nothing new, but then I accidentally scroll back to her albums and find one labelled "M" that appears to be locked.

I unlock it with her thumbprint, and loads of images and videos pop up of me, us, the family who raised us, and I spend the next hour swiping through them. She was always taking pictures or recording me. She even has pictures of newspaper clippings from my arrest, the headline that my sister testified, that I nearly broke my lawyer's face when he told me Olivia had turned her back on me.

I didn't hold back when she was in that witness box—my interpreter translated everything I signed. I let the world know how much of a whore my sister was, how she was always on her knees for me, that Mom sold her virginity, fucking everything, but I was silenced and labelled as a madman, though I refused to plead insanity.

Those few days of the trial were like a blur. I was so mad at Olivia, but I do kinda regret letting it all out. Not that anyone believed me—again, madman and all. But what we had was real. We fucked, maybe in a little bit of a messy situation, but we'd covered all boundaries, and I was fully prepared to tell everyone what she meant to me, but then the cops came, and it ended.

I waited for her in that cell—day after day. But it's okay now, because I'm here.

I grin as I shut off her phone and stare at the ceiling, my hand behind my head. Despite everything, I got to have sex with my sister again. It only took nearly a fucking decade.

Turning on my side, I open her drawer and pull out her journal. Total invasion of privacy, but it allows me to see into her head without needing to split open her skull and inspect her brain with a magnifying glass.

She touches a lot on sexual activity—how inactive she is, which makes me smile. After tonight, we are officially actively fucking, my sweet Olivia. I'll be doing this every single night now. She came all over my cock, whimpered my name, and moaned, so she definitely liked it.

What kind of a brother would I be if I didn't give her more?

A few times, she's mentioned the guy across the street—me by the way. She writes about watching me, wondering what I look like without my helmet, and once, she wrote she thinks it could be me but quickly backtracked, because if it was me, surely the last thing I'd be doing is living across the street and giving her space—if it was me—then she'd probably be dead.

Ridiculous—I don't want to kill her; I want to crush her. There's a difference.

She wants to gather enough courage to talk to the biker. She wants to give him her number and somehow ask him out. Which, again, is fucking hilarious and annoys the shit out of me, because she has no idea who he is. He could be a ninety-year-old man or have a face covered in warts, or worse, the biker could look like that fuckwit Parker.

In her recent journal entries, she talks about being lonely and that the marriage Mom's set up terrifies her. She doesn't find her future husband attractive from all the photos Mom emailed her and thinks he'll most likely cheat on her like her brother did.

Firstly, I didn't cheat. And secondly, we weren't in a relationship either. I was her secret little fuckboy; someone she could teach what she loved.

My eyes fall on the stack of letters I wrote to her—she has them strapped together with a rubber band in the drawer. Some of them are severely crumpled. As if she's gotten mad and scrunched them up, only to try flattening them once again.

I drop her journal and pull the top one out and unravel it. It's the first one I ever sent her. I read over it, shaking my head at my idiotic younger self.

Words like "missing you" and "I didn't think it was possible to be without you, and now there's a huge wall between us" and "will you visit me? I'm sorry for yelling at court" and my least favorite, a very dark time for me, "I'm not comfortable around these people. They call me a weirdo like the kids at school did because I won't talk. Please don't leave me in here," yet she didn't reply, even when my letters grew more desperate. No reply. Not to this letter, or the one after, or the fifty-odd after that.

I even begged her in some of these letters, demanding to know why she hadn't come to see me, if I'd done something wrong. I was in a state of confusion for so long, wondering—no, calculating—what error I'd made in the last few years.

I even told her, in a very messy letter—one of my last—that I had no idea how to control the way I felt about her, and that if I had got her pregnant, I'd step up even though I had no idea how to be a good father, that if she'd visit with my son or daughter, let me see them, I'd do better.

She didn't reply to that one either.

I must've been a depressed asshole.

I twist to look at my girl, my little sister, and brush my fingers through her hair. I hope she isn't sore tomorrow, but at the same time, I hope she's in fucking agony.

When she wakes, she'll be confused, probably think she had a bad dream, and I'll be watching her, either from the shadows or behind my computer screens, waiting for the next opportunity to strike.

CHAPTER 12
MALACHI

Olivia: *What time does the festival start?*
    Abigail: *Seven, I think. Are you still sick? Please tell me you aren't gonna cancel???*
Olivia: *I'm not.*

I smirk while I read the messages between my sister and her friend. She'd woken up yesterday, clouded and a little unsure of her surroundings, and staggered to the bathroom. I'd held my breath in case I hadn't put the small rug in the right place, but she just relieved herself and showered.

Her confusion continued when she saw the empty sink and trashcan, then she sat on her sofa and massaged the inside of her thighs, the same ones I was between. She'd pressed her palm to her forehead, and through the feeds in my apartment, I'd watched her search the internet for answers as to why her thighs were sore—but none of the results filling the screen were the right one.

The reason you're sore, and the reason your thighs are a little bruised, is because I fucked you, Olivia. And you loved it. It won't be the last time either, little sister. I will fuck you again. And again. And again, until you lose your voice the way I did and silently cry until you realize you still love me.

I keep smiling. I also keep talking to myself in my head as if my sister is in there, trapped within the darkness of my mind—it satiates me a little to imagine it; to believe she can hear everything I'm thinking, even though it would take me an hour minimum to actually get those words out.

Maybe I am a little insane.

Another message comes through—Olivia saying she's leaving work early and will head to Abigail's house to get ready before they go to the festival. It's in the middle of nowhere, an abandoned barn on a farm that's now a designated party place all year round.

I hum to myself as I watch Olivia walking home on my screens—which annoys me because she has a perfectly functional car in the apartment garage. Why walk and show everyone your perky tits in that tight dress and your peachy ass? Why smile at someone when they walk past you? Why are you not smiling at me?

When I notice my cigarettes are nearly done, I get dressed, pull on my black hoodie and combats, and grab my motorbike helmet on the way out the door. I keep the monitoring software open on my phone as I walk down the flights of stairs, refusing to take the elevator because I'll lose my signal. I flick through the various feeds, trying to find her, and when I reach the front door, I slip on my helmet and walk out.

My bike is parked right outside. It's new—a black Kawasaki imported from Japan. Fast as fuck and beautiful to look at. It's my pride and joy—after Olivia obviously.

I freeze when my eyes lift to find my main goal in life walking right towards me. Her hair flows in the wind, eyes bright, and her hand is wrapped around a basket filled with fruit.

Wait. She's heading straight for me.

Fuck. My visor isn't see-through, is it?

No. I made sure it wasn't.

Can she see my tattoos?

She has no idea I got one on my neck, right?

Fuck, why am I sweating?

She has that cute grin on her face as she walks up to the side of my bike, her eyes dancing under the mop of hair hidden beneath the hood of her coat—she's just pulled it up to shield herself from the rain now drizzling from the sky.

Seeing her up close, conscious and not through a screen, or in my goddamn dreams, knocks the air out of my lungs. As does knowing that there might be a trace of my cum inside her still, that her milky thighs are tender—fucked and fucked and fucked.

Does she know it's me? Has she figured out that I screwed her while she was asleep? Fuck, I don't know. I'll just look at—

"Hey," she says, her voice like music to my depraved ears. "Do you live nearby? I always see your bike parked here."

Mmmhmm, go away, Olivia, before I crush your windpipe. Or worse, fuck you in public with your stupid basket of fruit rolling down the street.

"My name is Olivia." She reaches out her hand, her cheeks reddening as she blushes. "I moved here a little over a year ago."

Can she fuck off? She's ruining my plan.

Her hand drops when I don't acknowledge her existence. "Oh, I'm sorry. I didn't mean to be intrusive. I'll just…" She turns around, going stiff as she looks for her last word. "Go."

But I don't want her to go.

Then again, I'll fuck up my words, and she might realize who I am.

And if Olivia finds out her darling brother is living across the street, stalking her like he has nothing else to do in his boring life, then she might disappear—or worse, call the cops again and get me charged with fuck knows what next.

Come on, Malachi, I urge myself. *Say something.*

"Kai," I say quietly. The fewer syllables, the easier it is to talk.

She stops and turns, confused.

I clear my throat, my lips moving a few times before I get the words out. "My name…" *Breathe, asshole.* "Kai."

She smiles wide. "Well hello, Kai."

Is she… flirting with me? Me?

No, she's flirting with a stranger. Not me.

Not fucking me.

I want to strangle her.

"Hi," I say, not bothering with her name because I'll fuck it up. At least I don't sound like an old man—my voice is quite deep and what people call "husky," and I know she likes that.

She smiles again and turns away, walking towards her apartment entrance. I stare at her ass, the sway of her hips, and wonder how long I can hold my breath before I die.

My bones are shaking—I think I might pass out as soon as she vanishes into the building. Being so close to her like this, with her bright eyes and mesmerizing smile, kinda knocks me off my fucked-up axis. I almost want to abort my revenge-fueled mission and tell her I forgive her, that we can be together now that I'm no longer seen as part of the Vize family—yet I still hold the surname on all my documents and bank accounts.

But she was flirting with me, not knowing who I am.

Why does that fuck me off so badly?

I climb onto my bike, turning the key and reveling in the vibrations all over my body. It's nearly as mind-bending as feeling Olivia come all over my cock. Seeing her on her knees on my balcony while Dad yells from beneath it. Fucking into her mouth—my first ever blowjob—and seeing my cum on her lips.

Tasting her for the first time with my mouth.

The kiss in her bed—the way she wanted me to grab her throat and choke her.

The way she cried while Dad was bleeding to death under her while I fucked her from behind.

Depraved thoughts have me fighting the urge to follow her into her home.

But then I see her again, heading straight for me with a piece of paper in her hand, and I frown when she reaches it out to me. It nearly blows away in the wind, but I catch it.

"I know this is forward, but I don't speak to many people." She hands me the paper. "This is my number, and this is where I'm going tonight. It's a Halloween festival just outside town. You should come."

"Thanks," I say, nearly hissing the word. "I'll…" I swallow, breathing through my nerves, trying to get this right. "I'll go."

"Really?" Her eyes widen. "Awesome! I can meet you outside the main gate at seven? Text me when you're there?"

I nod, and she blushes again before heading back to her apartment. I want to crack her skull open and feed her the gray matter of her brain, because what the fuck is she doing inviting a stranger out?

She's annoying me at the same time as making me nervous. She's basically asked me—someone she's never seen without a helmet—on a date. I could be an ugly motherfucker, a predator, or a murderer, and she's just given me a free invitation to meet with her.

I'm a little lost when it comes to socializing and living normally, but are we not a little old to be going to festivals like this? It's more like a rave with a fairground that teenagers usually swarm. I'm twenty-eight, nearly twenty-nine, and I'm sneaking around, fucking my sister, and planning on going to a Halloween party to chase her into the darkness and fuck her some more.

I mean, I'll go, but the idea of her so easily flirting with someone has me crushing the paper with her number, squeezing my throttle, and speeding down the street.

I glare at my phone—the new phone I had to go buy because I can't use my own one. She still has my number after all these years, so she'd know it's me.

Me: *Hey, it's Kai.*

I roll my eyes at myself. Out of all the fucking names, I picked what people tried to use as my nickname? I hate it. It was either that or Vizey growing up, and I hated both. My name is Malachi, nothing else.

I'm surprised she didn't put two and two together and realize who I was.

The stranger on a motorbike she just flirted with and asked out without knowing who she was talking to.

The phone dings, and I lean back on my bed with my towel around my waist, water droplets sliding down my chest. I just did a workout and ran on my treadmill for far too long, needing to expel some energy before tonight, but I still feel like there's a lot more left to give.

Olivia: Hi! I didn't think you would reach out. Are you coming tonight?

Am I so far from reality that I have no idea how to reply? Do I just simply reply "yes" and that's it? How do I keep the conversation going? Do I ask her if she's interested in sex? If she's just looking for a friend? If her pussy is still tender from being pounded on her bathroom floor?

Me: Yeah. 7?

There. Simple and fine and in no way suspicious, right?

I glance over at my desk, my eyes zoning in on her sitting on her sofa, knees tucked up, chewing her fingernails while staring at her phone. She types but stops and throws her head back, as if she's unsure what to say.

Smirking, I go sit at my desk and watch her fight her own

strange little battle. It absolutely does not help my stiffening cock that she's also in a towel, and that with her knees up, I can see between her legs.

When she still doesn't reply, still fighting her demons, I type again.

Me: *Are you single?*

She bites the corner of her lip as she grins, a blush creeping up her throat and cheeks.

Olivia: *My boyfriend would be furious if he knew I gave my number to some random biker.*

My smile drops, and my brows knit together. She's... not single? Since fucking when?

Olivia: *I'm kidding. I'm not a very funny person. But yes, I'm as single as they come. How about you?*

Technically, she's half single. She's neglected to mention that Mom's lined her up with a husband. She also has a brother—me, by the way—who she has a fascination with. I can be cocky about that—she does have pictures of me on her phone, and I have more than enough voicemails as proof.

She fancies me but flirts with the biker?

Me: *I don't do relationships.*

I grimace at my own words. I sound like a knock-off Christian Grey, without the whips and red room of sexual pain. Plus, I'm not a billionaire. I shake my head. Olivia made me watch all three movies back-to-back one night when we were teens, and

I hated it, but I loved watching her watch someone get fucked.

Olivia*: What do you do then?*

I drug my sister nearly every night, cuddle her in her unconscious state, clean her apartment, and one time, I stuck my cock in her. I probably shouldn't say that though.

Me*: What do you think?*

Olivia*: My imagination is a little crazy. I'll probably overstep and make you uncomfortable if I say what I think.*

This is taking a different direction. My little whore of a sister is trying to dirty talk the biker—me, her brother.

Me*: Maybe my imagination is crazier?*

My gaze is fixed on the screen, the one on my desk, as I watch her chest rise and fall, her knees falling open. Is she... turned on? That easily?

Olivia*: Prove it.*

Again, I'm annoyed, even though my dick is hard. She's trying to invoke sex from someone she doesn't know. She's parting herself with her small fingers and rubbing her clit on her sofa, and I'm tossing aside my towel to fist my cock, watching her find pleasure.

Pleasure she wants from a stranger.

I let go of my dick and type, refusing to come unless it's on or in her.

Me*: See you at 7.*

The gas mask sits comfortably on my face as I stare at myself in the mirror. With my black combats and black hoodie, the hood pulled up, she'll never know it's me.

I flip a screwdriver in my hand as I watch her through my screens—she's curling her hair as she sits in front of the floor-to-ceiling mirror at her friend's house. Is it normal to walk around naked in front of your friend? Abigail, disgustingly, only has panties on, and I try to block her from my vision as Olivia finishes her hair and rubs cream all over her naked body.

I imagine her friend chopped up as she rubs the cream onto Olivia's back. When she disappears into the bathroom, my sister fixes her makeup, so her lashes are too long, and paints on black lipstick to go with her goth-bride costume.

Her heels are too high—she still won't be anywhere near as tall as me, but how will she run in them? The game will be over before it properly starts.

The stockings cover her legs to her thighs, and the corset pushes her tits up, the train of the veil streaming down to her ass.

She's not smiling at herself in the mirror as she inspects her art—because that's what Olivia Vize is, a piece of fucking art I want to own. I do own. She just doesn't know it yet.

She looks sad. It could be the hour she spent crying to her friend about me, or while she watched videos of us, or the research she did online that—once again—gave her nothing.

She takes pictures in the mirror, faking smiles from different angles, then she tosses her phone on the bed and sits at the foot of it. There's music playing in the background, another Taylor Swift song, and she's miming the words while she waits on her friend.

I grin when I see the necklace she's wearing—the locket with our pictures in it. It fits with her costume, looking old and rustic. I watched her clip it on earlier, and she stared at the photo of us inside for longer than necessary.

You see how good we are together, Olivia? We could've had the world, and you had to ruin it. I was going to give you everything you ever wanted. Now I need to take. *I nearly have all of you.*

I have your mind.

I have your body.

I have your soul. The fear I instill in you. The pain I inflict when you defy me.

You have a black heart, little sister, but I'll own that soon too.

Olivia and her friend leave the house, heading to the festival. It's not too far—I've been reading articles about it online. There will be dancing, fairground rides, food, and alcohol, and there's a corn field that stretches all the way to the woods. I fully intend to make use of that space.

I flip the screwdriver in my hand a few times then tuck it into my back pocket, checking to see if my motorbike helmet fits over my mask, but it doesn't, so I chuck it aside and settle on using the gas mask instead.

It's eight by the time I get there. I intentionally made myself late, made her blow my phone up while I watched her through the crowds. She's sexy—far sexier than watching her through the screens. She's dancing, drinking spirits, her and her friend laughing and throwing their heads back to the music. She keeps checking her phone for a reply from me, but she won't get one.

Abigail's mouth is latched to a stranger's, and Olivia goes to get another drink, checking her phone on the way. I stay behind her, my hands fisting at my sides when I see the way people are looking at her. At how fucking hot she is.

If I had a gun, I would've put a bullet in at least ten people's heads by now.

With the gas mask on, she won't recognize me. Not as the biker, and not as her brother. I stay close behind, watching as she pays for another drink, sipping it as she walks off to the side. Her heels click on the concrete, the sound softening as she carefully leaves the dancing side of the festival and heads towards the fairground.

Some of the costumes are impressive, and some are downright ridiculous. Before I was in prison and shut off from the world, I never saw the big deal about Halloween, but my sister has always loved it. She likes to be scared, and I guess the entire theme of this holiday is to be scary.

Fine, I'll be scary.

She rounds the corner, and I see my opportunity to pounce. I pull the screwdriver out from my back pocket, closing the distance between us and grabbing the hair at the back of her head, then I press the screwdriver into her back and shove her between two broken tractors.

Olivia screams, but it's muffled as I cover her mouth. "Shhhhh," I whisper against her ear, spinning her around and slamming her back against the tractor wheel. I hold the screwdriver to her throat, and her pupils are expanding, her breaths uneasy, but the glaze in her eyes tells me she's enjoying this.

I tilt my head. "Kai," I say, and she relaxes a little. "This," I start, digging the point of the screwdriver against her pulse, "is what I do."

Will she notice how broken my words are? How badly I say them?

She bites her lip. "Hmm. What now?"

I smirk under the gas mask, easing off her neck and dragging the screwdriver down her chest, scraping her skin.

She's never heard my voice as Malachi. She can't see my face or my hair color or any of my tattoos with my gloves on. The only thing this version of me has in common with my true self is my height.

I stare at her for a moment. So beautiful. So fucking mine. "I'll give you a head start." My voice is rough, but I somehow manage to say those words without stuttering or overthinking the articulation of each syllable. I tip my head towards the cornfield. "Run, little stranger."

Run. I wonder if she'll remember throwing that word at me all those years ago. But if it triggers any memories for her, she doesn't show it. I step back, my pants tenting with my thickening cock as she takes a deep breath and disappears into the cornfield.

I count to five, ten, fifteen, twenty, and flip the screwdriver in my hand before I chase after her.

Fuck, she can run.

I forgot Olivia used to be a cheerleader and has the stamina of a long-distance runner.

Her heels lie discarded in the middle of the field, and I can hear her little gasps of breath the further we get from the festival. Spooky music plays, the cackling laugh of a monster, and I hear her yelp as she trips over something.

I stop behind tall crops of corn, panting as I grip the screwdriver in my hand. She pushes herself back up to her feet, spinning left and right, wondering which direction would be best. The woodland isn't far. I could drag her in there, but I quite like this setting. She looks terrified, but also eager, like she wants me to catch her.

The stranger.

Whacking hair from her face, she turns and runs further away from the music, and I smirk as I take careful steps, letting her go further and further, until I pick up my pace. My boots are heavy on the fallen corn, and I see her glance over her shoulder, spot me, and then her eyes widen as she screams loudly.

Damn, my cock is solid, and I didn't think Olivia could go any faster, but I'm mistaken. Even dressed the way she's dressed, I need to up my speed to catch her.

My hand fists the back of her veil, twisting into her hair, and she shrieks as I throw her to the side, making her roll over the snapped crops. Instantly, she starts crawling on her hands and knees to try to get away from me.

I grab her ankle, and she kicks me in the face, nearly knocking my mask off. She tries to crawl forward again, but I groan in annoyance and grab her nape, forcing her face into the dirt while I position myself behind her. She slaps at me from behind, but her attempts are useless as I rip off her panties, pocket them, and pull my screwdriver back out.

She goes stiff as I run the sharp, flat tip up her inner thigh, digging it in enough to cause a thin tear on her sensitive skin. Little beads of blood trickle down her thigh.

She's still, but I can hear her breath hitching as I move the tip to her other thigh.

Her ass is in the air, and I push her poor excuse for a skirt up her back, exposing her to me, and she winces as I let a gathering of spit drip from my mouth, under my mask, landing on her back hole.

She shakes, pushing back against me as I pull the screwdriver away from her thigh, leaning over her body. I let go of her nape and grip her hair, tipping her head back. "Open," I demand, pressing the handle of the screwdriver to her lips. She parts them, taking the handle into her mouth and flattening her lips. "Suck."

My cock threatens to rip through my combats as it presses against her, but I refuse to let it free. This is about her right now, and I'm going to make her cry.

I want to make her sob in both pleasure and pain. With fear and horror.

No one can see us way out here—the crops are taller than me, and the music playing is faint. I can hear her heaving through her nostrils as I sink the handle of the screwdriver deeper into her throat, gasping as I pull it from her pretty mouth and slide myself back onto my haunches.

Her pussy is soaked, drenched in her arousal, her ass puckered with my spit. I lick my lips, taking careful breaths as I drag the handle up her thigh, over her ass, then back down to her pussy. I tease her opening, her clit, making her whimper and push herself back for more.

"Kai," she moans. "Please."

Kai. Not Malachi. She's moaning another man's fucking name.

Then I see her face, the way she looked at me when she told everyone how violent I was, how she wanted to be free of me, how she was scared of me. My anger builds, and I force the handle into her ass instead.

She cries out, lunging forward, but I hold her in place with a large palm on her back.

Her ass grips the screwdriver, and I push it in more, until her greedy hole devours the full handle. Then I let go of it, watching her pulse around the metal trapped there.

"Kneel," I order, my voice a little rough.

I get to my feet as she glances at me over her shoulder, her eyes wide and wild, the screwdriver hanging out of her ass. She winces as she sits up, a tear sliding down her cheek, and I unbuckle my belt, gripping her hair and dragging her in front of me. "Kneel."

"Fuck you," she snaps, whimpering as she gets to her knees. "Can I take it out?"

I slap her across the face, grip her jaw, and free my cock. "No."

More tears slip out, and the sight of them makes my head throb. Both heads. But mostly the one pressing against her lips. "Open."

Momentarily, I pause. What if she sees my piercings and realizes it's me? Maybe it's too dark for her to see? She'll definitely feel them in her throat.

I have no fucks left to give at this moment, maybe later.

She opens her mouth, and I don't give her a second to adjust before I fist my hands in her hair and thrust fully into her mouth, making her gasp around my cock, her throat constricting around the girth, the piercings up the underside of my cock reacquainting themselves with her tongue.

The warmth, the fucking wetness of her throat as I force myself deep, using my grip on her hair to fuck my hips forward, choking her.

Her hands fly up to my thighs, trying to push away, but I don't stop or ease off—I thrust harder, faster, knocking her back a little and making the screwdriver go deeper into her ass.

My balls tingle, slapping her chin as I rock my hips, my head thrown back on a deep growl. She swallows around my dick, sucking, licking, and I pause for a moment and look down at her taking over.

Her eyes are on me, her mascara smeared down her cheeks, black lipstick on my dick. She's crying, but she's also rocking her own hips, enjoying her ass being pummeled by the screwdriver. My balls tighten, and as she hums around my thickness, I screw my eyes shut and shove her off me, making her scream when she lands on her back.

185

I climb on top of her, kick her legs apart, and force my cock into her. The tip of the screwdriver is an inch from my balls, and as I cover her mouth and grab her throat, leaning up so she can watch me in the gas mask, I thrust all the way to the hilt, drawing a painful moan from her.

So pretty, so fucking violent as she slaps at the hand robbing her of air, digging her nails into my skin. She goes rigid as I hammer my cock into her like I'm trying to kill her, hard enough to hurt, fast enough that she must be seeing stars.

"Such a whore," I groan, the words broken but effective as she glares at me before her eyes roll. "Take it. Fucking take it."

She's clenching around me, and it takes me mere minutes of fucking her before she tenses everywhere and screams against my palm as her orgasm smashes into her.

I follow immediately, filling her with every drop of my cum, watching her drift in and out of consciousness from my grip on her throat, her eyes wide from the strangling pressure, her body starting to go limp beneath me.

She just let a stranger fuck her.

Why does that piss me off?

I release her neck and mouth, pressing my hands to the fallen crops by her head, still sliding my cock in and out of her despite it only being semi-hard.

I want to tell her she's beautiful, that she takes my cock so well, that she was fucking made for me. But I have no idea how to form those words properly without fucking them up, and it only makes me furious with myself and her.

She tries to say something, but she doesn't get to talk. I don't want to hear her voice right now.

I pull the cloth from my pocket, the one I already doused with chloroform, and hold it to her mouth while she fights me.

Sleep, beautiful sister.

My cock is still buried deep inside her, shallow thrusts until she passes out completely.

I snatch my mask off and toss it aside, shaking my head and breathing. Fuck, it's hot in there, and the sweat in my hair is getting itchy.

I pull my shirt up a little and look between us, watching my cock still sliding in and out, inch by inch, both our orgasms leaking from her cunt as I slip out. I gather up what I can from her thigh, and my eyes close on a groan as I sink two fingers into her heat. Keeping my seed inside her is a must—I've imagined it too many times to be healthy.

I don't want to get her pregnant—fuck that—but I like the idea of her being full of my cum. To know that it'll be dripping down her thighs.

I pull the screwdriver out of her ass, her still body making no movements, tuck it back into my pocket with the cloth, and sigh.

She has blood on her thighs. I cut her with the screwdriver, but they're not deep gashes—little cuts I lean down and lick clean. The taste of her coppery blood has me licking my lips, needing to taste more. I bite down hard on her other thigh, splitting her skin, and my eyes roll as I taste her blood there too.

I think I'm taking the Halloween spirit too seriously. I'll turn into a fucking vampire if I keep drinking her blood.

Pressing a kiss to her cunt, I slip my tongue through her hole and taste us both, then I suck a little on her clit and give it a chaste kiss.

Getting her on my bike is going to be a nuisance. I stand up, looking around, and when I spot a fence area near the road, I form a plan.

After covering Olivia's body with fallen crops, I grab my mask and put it on halfway, then leave her in the cornfield and head back to the festival, grabbing a beer from one of the stalls while I walk to my bike. Smoking, I wait a few minutes before I drive up the side of the field, parking close enough that I'll be able to carry her there safely.

I kick aside the corn and carry my unconscious sister to my bike, wanting to punch myself in the dick for not bringing my helmet to put on her. I keep her in front of me, my hand slipping down to touch her exposed pussy rubbing on my seat while I drive to an old farmhouse I bought a few weeks ago. Specifically for this moment with Olivia in my possession.

Surprisingly, she doesn't fall off, and when I reach the dark, narrow road, I smile at the thought of all the fun we're going to have here. Of the fear I'm going to instill in her when she realizes who's kidnapped her.

My little captive for the foreseeable future. My darling Olivia.

You aren't leaving here without me getting my revenge, you traitorous fucking bitch.

CHAPTER 13

MALACHI

W hy did her biological mom need to give her such a difficult fucking name?

Out of the millions of names she could have chosen, she picked one with four goddamn syllables? Did she not think of all the people out there who would struggle? The ones who need speech therapists or just settle on using sign language?

If her mom wasn't already dead, I'd kill her for calling her fucking Olivia.

I stare at the letters, tracing my finger over them. "O-liv-a," I say, shaking my head. "O-lay-ve-a."

I grit my teeth. Why the fuck can't I say it properly? I know how to say her name, but when I try to sound out the letters, my tone shifts, and I fuck it up.

What if I shortened it? She thinks my name is Kai. My real name is Malachi, by the way, not Kai, but she thinks that. What if I called her Liv?

"Liv," I say, grimacing. "Oli…via."

Closer.

I sit up straight and puff my chest and try to say it all as one word. "Ol-i-vara."

My confidence drops. Fuck off.

I scrunch up the paper, toss it in the trashcan, and light a cigarette, filling my lungs with the smoky poison while I watch my sister through my phone screen. She's hanging from the basement ceiling, chains on each wrist, a collar around her throat, ankles shackled with a spreader keeping her legs apart. She looks beautiful in her little goth-bride costume with her panties shoved into her mouth.

She's been hanging there for hours while I made sure our bedroom was ready. It is, and I can't wait to share the bed with her.

I pull on a black balaclava, chewing on some gum as I look in the small, cracked mirror on the wall. She might recognize my eyes, so I put the gas mask over the top of the balaclava, slide my gloves on, and head down to the basement with a sandwich and glass of water.

My heart rate spikes when I open the door to the basement and see her, even though she's out cold, her mascara and black lipstick smeared all over her pretty face.

I place the plate down and stand in front of her, tipping

her chin back and pulling the panties from her mouth. She breathes, her eyes fluttering, and I smile at her—not that she can see me—and bring the glass of water to her lips.

She gulps down each drop, and I wipe my gloved thumb over her lips and down to the collar on her throat. I was going to attach her to my cock or my wrist, but I want to give her some free will, for her to *want* to come to our bedroom with me. Just not yet. She hasn't earned it yet.

Her eyes open properly, and she sucks in air as the realization that she's chained up and stuck in place hits. "What the fuck?" she croaks. She looks down at her legs, at the spreader keeping them wide open. "Let me go!"

I shake my head and gather the sandwich in my hand, bringing it to her mouth. "Eat," I demand. "It's… good."

I clear my throat, annoyed with myself for fumbling a little on my words. She clamps her mouth shut, so I pinch her nose and shove the sandwich in when she finally parts her lips for air.

You need to eat, darling sister, or this will end sooner than planned. You need to stay healthy, hydrated, and well fed, while I make you suffer for stealing eight years from me.

I mean, I want to say that to her, but I have no idea how.

Instead, while she chews on the sandwich, I lower my free hand to her cunt, gliding my fingers through the wetness there. Always so wet. Fear always turns her on. And pain. I know between her legs and her back hole must be sore, and her jaw probably is too from how harshly I fucked her mouth.

She whimpers around the sandwich as I slip a finger inside her.

It's been around ten hours since we left the festival. I already sent messages to her friends to say she went home with her biker friend and that she'd reach out soon. I also saw an opened email from Mom with details for her first date with Xander.

My dear sister should be meeting her future husband tomorrow, but it's a shame she'll be sucking her brother's dick instead.

I add another finger, and she tenses everywhere. "Hmm," I hum, forcing the rest of the food into her mouth to gag her then slowly unclipping the front of her corset. Each clip makes her tits spill out the top, and when I get enough of them undone, she's writhing in the chains, trying to rock her hips into my hand, while I pinch her nipple.

I twist it, and she screams around the sandwich, spitting it out and gasping, "Please. Please."

I pull my fingers out of her and walk towards the small table, lifting a knife next to the plate, and I twirl it in my hand as I turn to her. She's crying again, her pussy soaking her thighs, and I smirk under my mask, blood rushing to my dick.

I walk behind her, and she fights against the chains to watch me, to see what I'm doing, but she's trapped. I clench my jaw to stop myself from severely hurting her, causing her more pain than she can handle, as I cut the rest of her corset off then press the point of the blade to her spine.

She trembles in only her skirt, the pathetic scrap of material easily ripped off with my hands and thrown aside too.

Her naked body has always been my heaven. Somewhere I don't belong, somewhere I shouldn't taint or cut, but as I walk round her and bring the sharp edge of the blade to her nipple, I slice carefully, making her stiffen everywhere as a trickle of blood slides down her stomach. I do the same to the other, and she moans in both pain and pleasure.

Her eyes land on me. "Take your mask off."

I shake my head, even though a shock of anxiety hits me. If she finds out it's me, what would she do? I'm having too much fun right now to ruin my hidden identity.

"If you take it off, I'll suck your dick."

I frown and stop walking around her. "What?"

My voice is deeper—a warning tone I've never heard from myself before.

She has no idea who I am, and she just offered to blow me in exchange for me taking off my mask. I clasp her chin in a firm hold, bringing the knife to her throat and pressing the sharp edge to her pulse. I want to slice it open, deep and gaping, to see her blood spill down her body. But I also want to kiss her, goddammit.

"I have a brother," she says, her eyes watering. "If you hurt me, he'll find you."

"Yeah?" The thrill going through me right now is fucking ecstatic. She just threatened me with myself—she thinks I'll save her.

My gaze drops to the locket sitting between her breasts, and she gasps as I snap it from her neck. "No!"

I open it, staring at the picture of our younger selves, shoving it in her face. "Him?"

"Y-Yes," she cries. "Please don't break it. *Please*."

"You love him?" My pronunciation stays firm.

"He's my brother," she replies, her bottom lip trembling. "Of course I love him."

I laugh—really fucking laugh, in a way I've never done before. My laughter is usually silent, a shake of my body while I smile, but this time it's loud, my head thrown back, a genuine grin on my face.

This fucking...

How can she say she loves me after destroying what we had?

I grip my mask and pull it off, and her face falls when she sees the balaclava. "A deal..." I stop, my tone already fucking up. "Is... a deal."

She watches me throw the gas mask aside, and I walk to the wall all the chains are connected to and loosen the ones on her wrists and collar, making her drop to her knees, her legs still parted wide from the spreader.

Her hair, if I wasn't wearing fucking gloves, would be so soft in my hold. I grip it while I stand in front of her.

The basement isn't bright, a shitty lamp to the side giving it a soft glow, so she can't see my piercings or eyes properly. I free my cock, grip her jaw firmly, and shove it into her mouth.

This time, I let her do the work. On her knees and in chains, the blood drying from her nipples, her pussy drenched, she wraps her slender fingers around the base of my cock and takes as many inches as she can. I'm not small and definitely not of average size, so the fact she can deep-throat my length is impressive.

I close my eyes and bask in the feeling of her sucking my dick, her other hand on my thigh, grasping, her throat contracting around my thickness. She chokes, but I grab the back of her head and hold her there until I feel myself getting close.

I don't want to finish yet, so I pull back and tuck my cock into my waistband, and tap her cheek with a light slap, chuckling as she glares at me.

"You're pierced."

I stare at her, not gracing her with a reply. Inside, I'm panicking. I don't have a normal piercing either. I have multiple, five bars like a ladder positioned up the underside of my cock and a hoop at the tip. I got my ears stretched a little when I got out of prison, tattoos on my neck and hands, but other than those changes since I was nineteen, nothing about me is different.

She wipes her mouth. "Give me back my locket."

Give me back my eight years, I want to say, but I ignore her.

She tries to stand on shaky legs and fails, so I help her by pulling the chain back into place, taking her off her feet completely. I wet my lips and grab a cigarette, watching her dangle from the ceiling, the collar choking her but not enough to kill her. She's gasping for air while I light a cigarette, inhaling and blowing the smoke against her pussy.

It clenches, and I smirk to myself as I bring my cigarette to her mound, just above her clit, and press the burning end to her skin. Only for a split second, but it's enough to make her scream a strangled scream—then moan as I drag my tongue up her glistening slit and suck on the area I just burned.

She's... aroused. More aroused.

So she likes that kind of pain too?

I leave a little trail of burns on her skin, all the way to her breasts and brand my initials just under them, and kiss and lick each mark until my cigarette is finished. I palm at her tits, biting her nipples and breaking skin, and her entire body trembles as an orgasm hits her. Her thighs are tense, and I watch her pussy clenching on thin air, her body rattling in the chains as I shove two fingers deep to bring her orgasm to its absolute peak.

She passes out right after, but I keep going. I lick at her clit, adding a third finger, fucking into her with them as I massage her ass.

Then I pull my fingers out and walk behind her to kneel, parting her ass cheeks with my hands and using the wetness from her cum to lube up her puckered hole. It's staring right at me, like it wants to have a conversation, so I silence it by burying my tongue inside.

She screams awake, and I grin to myself as I drag one last orgasm out of her.

This is going to be so fun, Olivia.

I'm sitting on my chair, waiting for her to wake up. It's been three hours, and I'm bored.

Standing, I grab another chain and hook it on the ceiling behind her, pulling it between her legs and ringing it through a hoop I installed to use as a pulley. I sigh, watching her for a minute, then yank the chain, making it ride between her legs and bring her off her feet.

The yelp she lets out makes me chuckle.

Her clit is trapped between two of the chain links, and I see a spot of blood. It looks good on her—red is definitely her color.

I lick the spot, and she flinches. "You fucking psycho!"

Good—fight back, little sister. Don't give in.

She tries to knee me in the face, but the chains stop her. I pull the chain between her legs higher, and she squeals, even though I can see how soaked she already is.

She's quite the masochist, and I love it, because I think I'm a sadistic bastard.

Olivia is biting back a moan as I drag my tongue up her ribs, stopping at her nipple. I suck on the tip, happy to see both nipples are already hard as stone. "You love pain," I say perfectly, and I want to pat myself on the back. "I love pain."

"Whatever, asshole," she snaps, pulling at her restraints. "You have no idea who you're messing with. When he finds out where I am, because he will, he'll come for you."

I smirk and tap her cheek. Stupid woman. Stupid, beautiful, smart woman I want to spend the rest of my life with.

On her tiptoes, she absently moves her hips forward, so the chain grinds against her pussy, and I sit back on my chair again and watch, lighting a cigarette. "Keep going," I demand, reaching under my waistband to fist my dick, stroking as she rubs herself over the chain.

It's rubbing against her ass too, and her eyes are rolling as she gives in. She's dirty, and fucking sexy, I'll give her that. I also want to fuck her back hole.

I stand and walk around her—she seems too engrossed in getting herself off, only pausing her hip movements when I step up behind her, parting her ass cheeks so I can watch the chain between them.

I reach forward and loosen the chain, hooking my finger through the links between her ass and moving it over one of her ass cheeks. It's still against her cunt, but now I have access to her ass.

I spit, the saliva rolling down her back to her hole, then shake my head and walk back to the table. I grab my knife, roll my sleeve up enough to show a little tattooed skin, and cut into my flesh as she gasps.

Behind her again, I let my blood trickle down her back, spreading it all over with my palm, watching it seep into the crevasse of her ass.

My cock is pulsing, and I pull it out, stroking it a few times with a bloody fist before lining up with her ass.

She fights against the chains again, but I don't hear her cries or moans or anything as I nudge the head of my cock into her back hole. Little by little, it grips me, and fuck, it's tight. Tighter than her cunt. I've never done this before, never fucked an ass, and I assumed it would be like sliding into Olivia's pussy.

I'm greatly mistaken. This is by far the best thing I've ever felt. It hurts with how narrow the tunnel of her ass is, clenching around each inch I manage to push in. She's crying, begging me—for what, I don't know. I'm more focused on how glorious it looks thrusting into her hole.

Blood is still trickling from my wrist, and I coat her back

with it then unfasten her collar and grab her throat, fucking her while the chains rub against her pussy.

She's shuddering in my hold, tears sliding against my hand as my blood stains her chest. Fuck, I can't see properly, and my moans are deep, loud, husky. I think I might need to stay in her ass forever.

It's official. I, Malachi Vize, hereby swear to be an ass man now. Forever and always, I will gratify my needs by burying my cock in my sister's tight back hole.

Her orgasm hits, and I can feel it in her ass. It gets tighter, so much so I fear my dick might get stuck or snap in half, but that's fine. I'd gladly die here.

Do you see this, Dad? I'm buried inside my sister again, and there's fuck all you can do to stop me.

My eyes roll to the back of my head as I fill her ass with my cum. I hold it there—deep, throbbing, pulsing each string of cum from my body—as she sobs her heart out, begging me to stop.

I lean forward and disconnect the chain, and she cries even more when I pull my cock out of her ass. I smile at my handiwork. The blood. The cum. The tears. I'm nearly finished here, and when I'm done, Olivia will swear herself to me forever.

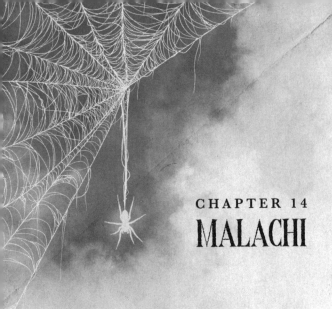

CHAPTER 14
MALACHI

Mom is trying to fucking annoy me.

First, she arranges for Olivia to have dinner with Xander. Now, she's emailing about setting a fucking wedding date for two weeks' time.

Maybe I should kill her. Would the wedding still go ahead if the mother of the bride had been tragically ripped apart and fed to a pack of wolves?

Knowing my family, probably.

My tarantula is crawling over my hand, and I watch him explore my scent. He's new. I bought him a few days ago, and I think he looks exactly like Spikey, my old pet—who Mom had destroyed when I was arrested.

They killed my fucking spider, the assholes.

I still want revenge for that too, because Olivia didn't even try to stop them—going by her journal, she didn't do much to stick up for me, only herself. In all honesty, everything I've read in that fucking book pissed me off. She talks about me a lot, about how abusive I was to her, yet she liked it. She liked when I was a manipulative dick and forceful.

Then why did you testify against me, sweet Olivia?

Why tell all those people what I did to Daddy then fill my phone up with voicemails of you crying and apologizing; why search for me when I was released?

Why act like you hate me when you miss me?

I'm a hypocrite. I internally rain havoc on any warm thoughts of Olivia, but deep down, I fucking missed her too. Being separated from her was like being thrown into the sea when you can't swim. Drowning—I was fucking drowning until I set eyes on my Olivia again.

She currently has some spider webs on her. My pet crawled all over her body until he decided to try to escape from the basement and made me chase the fucker.

"Ol-ivi-a," I mutter to myself. I try to whisper it faster and mess up. I sigh and check her phone for any new messages, but even her social media is dead. *Where has your exciting life gone, sister?*

The chains rattle, and I lift my gaze to see her waking up. "Ah," I start. "Good. You awake."

I meant to say "You're awake" but I guess I'm still learning that shit.

I stand and walk towards her while my spider scurries around my palm. He's still a baby, furry, but the way she's widening her eyes tells me that, one, she has no idea she has webs in her hair and on her body, and two, she's still terrified of anything with eight legs.

Poor little guy. He just wants to be understood, just like me. *Don't you, buddy?*

"Don't you dare come near me with that thing!"

I smile, still in my balaclava. I fucked her ass all of yesterday, and while she passed out, I went for a sleep in our bed and showered. I tried to sponge wash her, but she got turned on, and I ended up fucking her ass again.

She even begged me to give her pussy attention, and I denied her of it.

I can't help but smile at her. She's beautiful—she has been since we were kids. I think since I met her in the airport, I knew how important she'd be to me, and when she learned sign language, and how to play "Happy Birthday" on the piano for me, I thought I was important to her too. Years passed, but I could never handle being far from her. I always wanted to kiss her and laugh with her, to lie in her bed and watch her sleep, sniff her fucking hair like the drug it is.

I was—technically—her brother. I'm still classed as one, I think. And as much as I wanted to be special to her, to be with her, I never wanted to be her brother. I wanted to be her first kiss, her first love, her first dance at Homecoming. I wanted to hold her hand and kiss her whenever I wanted. I was never normal enough for her—the freak without a voice.

Our parents hated me—I was the adopted kid they never should've signed for. She was the angel—still is to me, despite everything—and I was the mistake.

My parents were already concerned about my fixation with my sister, but when I was fifteen, I kissed her during a board game and was moved to the other side of the manor, so we had to risk our lives every time we wanted to sneak into each other's room by walking across the roof ledge.

When I was nineteen, I knew the way I felt about Olivia was wrong. It was like an illness I had no idea how to treat. Olivia Vize was my sister, and I had fantasies of fucking her, of kissing her until we couldn't breathe, of me hurting her and her liking it.

I was so dangerously obsessed with her that I planned to fuck her in her sleep, but I settled for going on a date instead to try to make her jealous.

That was my first mistake—everyone made up lies about me. I was the loser, the weirdo, yet all the girls wanted to suck my dick or try to make me fuck them to see if I'd moan their name. I never went near Anna. I didn't kiss her, and I definitely didn't fuck her. Olivia was my first—she's the only person I've ever been with.

I tried to tell Olivia, but she kept grabbing my hands when I was signing, and I couldn't say her name, never mind all those words. She slapped me, yelled at me, then I got sensory overload and snapped.

And I guess I saw red and ruined it all.

Now, my sister is pulling away from me, as far as she can in her chains, while I drag my palm over her tits, my creepy-crawly spider settled on top of my hand. She's shaking so much, and her little whimpers are making my dick hard. I fix it in my pants, tucking it up into my waistband, and she glances down.

"W-Wait…" She hesitates, and the look in her eyes tells me this is a fear she may not get off on. Good thing this isn't about her—this is for me. For the years she took from me.

I tilt my head the way I always do when I look at her and drag my palm up and over her web-covered breast to her throat.

She freezes all over as I let the spider crawl onto her face.

I don't think she's even breathing as I tilt my head further, watching it scurry over one of her eyes. "Beau-ti-ful."

"Pl-Please take it off. Please, Kai. Please. I'll do anything."

I capture my lip between my teeth and walk behind her. "I like the way—" I stop, gathering my courage to keep the words coming, sinking my teeth into her neck to buy me some time. She whimpers and pulls on the chains. "You scream," I finish, licking a trail from her collarbone, over her nape, and biting the other side of her neck.

I move her hair over to the other shoulder, tugging down my pants to free my cock, and press it to her entrance. "Scream louder," I add as I force my cock into her pussy from behind, and her lungs expel the most arousing fucking sound, her head thrown back.

My pet is crawling up the side of her face, and I can see the fear in her expression—it makes me chuckle.

"The itsy bitsy spider," I whisper against her ear, sliding in and out of her cunt. "Climbed up the waterspout."

My tone is surprisingly good, considering. Maybe it's the fact I'm distracted by my body pressed against hers, or the way her pussy clutches at my cock as I keep thrusting, her breaths gasping out of her in both fear and pleasure.

"Down came the rain," I say slowly, biting my lip and groaning as I get deeper into her depths. "And washed... the spider... out."

"Oh God," she moans, the chains rattling as she pulls at them just as my little furry friend crawls up into her hair.

"Out came the sun," I whisper, dropping my hand down the front of her to pinch her clit while I twist her nipple. "And dried up... all the rain."

I feel my spider scurry onto my neck, settling there as I fuck my girl with more force, a shiver shooting down my spine to my balls as I force out the rest of the lyrics through gritted teeth. "The itsy... bitsy... spider..."

She explodes around my cock, her inner walls clenching my thickness, and I pinch her clit harder, thrusting deeper and making her scream through her orgasm.

My balls tighten more than they ever have, and I still inside her, my cock pulsing strings of cum with each twitch of my own release.

My vision blurs, and I nearly collapse against her as I catch my breath.

She goes limp again, and I sigh and pull out, pressing my forehead to her back as I spread the sticky substance leaking from her over her cheeks, slapping one hard enough to leave a mark.

The tickling at my nape where my balaclava isn't covering has me carefully reaching back for my tarantula.

I hold him in my palm and chuckle as I grab a chain above me for support, since I'm a little dizzy. "Climbed up… the spout again."

He crawls up my arm while I circle my sister.

I go to smell her hair and frown. It doesn't smell like strawberries like it did when we got here. The burns look like they could use more cream too. And her wrists are all red and raw from the chains.

Have I had her chained up for too long?

I've been more than happy to clean her up when she wet herself, feed her when she needed food, but I think my girl needs a good scrub. She's covered in dried blood, webs, cum, cigarette burns, and bite marks.

Fine.

Maybe she's had enough.

I know I have. I kind of want to just lie with her—cuddle her, even if she hits me in the process.

I free her wrists and catch her in my arms. My spider sits on my shoulder as I carry her out of the basement. I let him come with us to the bedroom while she snores against my chest, lifting her higher so I can flop her over my shoulder then settling my pet into his tank.

I take Olivia into the bathroom and fill the tub while I sit her on the ground, her back to my front, and run a comb through her hair. She's whimpering in her sleep, rubbing her thighs together, so I lower my hand and cup her pussy, and instantly, the greedy little stranger pushes against my palm.

"Nope," I say, taking it away. "Not yet."

I lift her into the tub, not climbing in behind her like I would whenever I drugged her at her apartment. I wash all the blood from her body with a sponge, then grab her usual shampoo brand and lather her hair with it. She keeps slipping under the water, and it's fucking annoying me.

Holding her in place, I strip my clothes with one hand— even the balaclava—and climb in behind her to keep her still while I wash her hair. I sigh in contentment at how perfectly she fits against me, palming her tits and tweaking her nipples, making her cry out softly.

She's still unconscious as I dry her off, brush her teeth, and kiss her, then place her in bed. I don fresh clothes—a hoodie and sweats to hide my tattoos—and pull on the balaclava again, sitting on the dresser with a cigarette while she sleeps.

Naked. Exposed. Branded with my mouth and my initials burned into her, and little cuts from my knife. She looks perfect. She looks like mine.

I stub out the smoke and climb into bed beside her, feeling tired myself, but I can't sleep—she'll wake before me and try to run away.

She can't leave me. Not again.

I pull my sister against me—the perfect little spoon, my puzzle piece—wrap my arms around her, and kiss the spot behind her ear. Soft, chaste kisses. She sighs into me, rolls her hips, and I lean back to watch her ass rub against my hardening cock.

I'm reminded of that first time, in my bed, when she thought I was asleep and rubbed her ass against my cock. I was so fucking close to pushing the limit at that point, but I was a virgin, and whether I was a cocky wanker or not, Olivia made me nervous.

She still does.

I push Olivia onto her back and settle between her legs, pulling my boxers down over my ass so my dick springs free. I fist the base, stroke it once, then tap it against her clit, making her tense and part her legs wider for me.

I glide my pierced head against her slick folds and ease it through her opening; she rolls into me, her pussy wrapping around my head and making me twitch.

I fist the pillow beside her head with one hand and grab her throat with the other, and her eyes ping open as I squeeze—just as I pummel one hard thrust into her.

Good girl, Olivia. Be fucking awake while I take you like this.

I haven't had her missionary with her awake, and I want her to look into my eyes while I fuck her.

Her widening gaze flicks between both of my eyes, and I bury my face in her neck as I rock my hips into her, slamming so hard, the headboard rattles against the wall. I inhale, smelling her hair, the freshness of it, and my cock tingles as it thickens.

"Malachi?"

CHAPTER 15
MALACHI

I pause, my lungs halting, my heart restarting as I stay still, as if I just imagined her saying my name. Did she? Or is it her voice in my head again? When I was locked up, I always had conversations with her, but never real ones. I was losing my fucking mind and deluded myself into thinking she was lying beside me some nights.

"Malachi," she says again, and I pulse inside her, pushing my arm straight so I can get off her.

But she traps me by wrapping her legs around my waist, her lips parted as she erratically looks at my eyes again. Her shaky hand lifts, and I don't pull away as she slides the balaclava over my chin, my mouth, my nose, then removes it completely.

My black hair, long and falling over my eyes, catches her attention. She brushes her hand through it, her legs still tightly wrapped around my hips as a tear slips from the corner of her eye.

Her gaze follows her fingers, dropping from my hair to trace one of my brows, down the side of my face to my jawline, grazing over the stubble to my lips.

Mesmerized.

Like she hasn't seen me in over eight years.

I mean, she hasn't, but I expected her to scream at me to get off her or hit me, to curse at me for what I've done—not to do… this. She's tracing my facial features.

I'm letting her. Instead of making her pay for ruining nearly a decade of my life, I'm letting her touch me so freely, and I love it.

I'm all warm and tingly and I… like it.

Her fingertips are soft. I've been so deprived of touch while being locked up that when her palm cups my cheek, I press against it.

"You can talk," she says, her bottom lip trembling. "You can… You can talk, Malachi."

I stare down at her, my lips moving but no sound coming out. I shake my head—then freeze all over when she lifts her head and kisses me. Her lips are so fucking smooth and addictive, and I relax into the kiss and part my lips, allowing her tongue to slip in to move against mine. Her taste, her fucking kiss—I had no idea I needed it so much.

She rocks her hips up, and I meet her movements with a slow thrust, both of us gasping into each other's mouth. She grabs a fistful of my hair and tilts my head to deepen the kiss while I slowly move in and out of her.

She's soaked, gripping my cock, but I'm more focused on her kissing me, the way she whimpers and fists my hair, the way she controls this as she pushes me off her and climbs on top of me.

Olivia looks like a fucking angel as she straddles my hips, lifting to her knees to hover over my cock then lowering herself so I fill her again. Her hands are on my chest, digging into the thick muscles there as she bounces on my cock. I hold her hips, fucking up into her cunt, gritting my teeth as a deep growl rips from my throat.

She cries out above me, her pussy gripping me like a fist as she slams down onto my thickness, scraping her nails down my chest as her inner walls clutch me through her orgasm. She's shaking but still bouncing on my cock, taking control as she drops and grinds.

"I want to hear you moan again," she says, leaning down to grab my throat, dropping her hips on me faster, making my eyes roll to the back of my head. "Let your little sister hear your voice. I want to feel the vibrations in your throat while you moan for me, Malachi."

Her forceful words, the way she cuts off my oxygen, and how hard she's slamming down on my cock makes my balls tighten. I came not long ago, what the fuck is happening?

I go dizzy as I let out another moan and grab her shoulder, keeping her still as I pulse every drop of cum deep inside her.

She collapses on top of me, and I hold her in my arms, my heart pounding in my chest, sweating between us, gasping to draw air into my lungs.

After about ten minutes, she sits up, looking down at me. "Jesus, Malachi. What the hell are you doing?"

She could be asking me a number of things here.

Why did you fuck me while I was unconscious?

Why did you shove a screwdriver in my ass?

The chains? The spider? The cuts and bites and burn marks?

So many questions, and all I can do is watch her above me, calling me by my name, willingly on my cock, and looking all beautiful and mine.

But then I remember our reality, and what she thinks I did to her years ago.

"Anna... lied," I force out, feeling the rage already coming when I think about that bitch and how I stupidly didn't snap her neck as soon as I was free.

"She lied?" Olivia asks, her brow furrowing.

I nod, twirling my finger around a lock of her hair. "You w-w-w..." I stop, shaking my head in annoyance. It was way easier to talk with my identity hidden.

"Take your time," she says, smiling down at me, capturing my hand as I pull it away from her hair and linking our fingers.

"I could listen to your voice all day. Just… breathe. I'm listening. Go slow."

"You w-were my first. I pr-promise. My… first and… my only."

At least she isn't laughing at the way my speech is. She's being patient.

"I had a feeling it was all lies. My friends went a little weird on me after the allegations about us, and our parents made me deny that we were ever intimate. I… hated you for what you did to Dad, but I missed you. I even had a feeling it was you all along, but I wanted you to punish me. You wouldn't have been locked away if it wasn't for me testifying."

Then she frowns and slaps my chest. "You put a damn spider on me, asshole!" She points at her body, the burned initials with raised brows. "Really? And what took you so long? You were released months ago."

I grin and lift my hands, signing, *I was waiting until the right time to show myself.*

She snatches my wrists and shakes her head. "No. Use your voice. Talk to me."

"I'm…" I stop, nervously licking my lips. "Not good at that."

"You were perfectly fine whispering a nursery rhyme in my ear while your monster crawled all over my body."

"You came," I say with a shrug. "You… liked it."

She grins wide. "It's so deep."

"Yeah." I lift my hands again. "Let me… s-s-sign this."

She nods and watches my hands.

I'm not sorry for beating up Dad. He made my life hell for no reason. I do miss Mom, though, and I know we have a little sister. She seems nice, but I don't plan on speaking to her.

"She is nice," she says. "I think you'd like her. She's quite talkative and full of energy."

Then I'd hate her.

She rolls her eyes. "You were the one leaving chocolates and flowers in my house?"

Yes, I sign. *I also fucked you while you were unconscious on your bathroom floor.*

"I'm going to pretend I didn't see you sign that."

You wrote in your journal that you wanted to experience somnophilia. You came on my cock and everything. Tick it off your little list.

She flattens her lips. "Fine. Where are we?" she asks, changing the subject.

This is our home. I'll renovate and decorate it. I knew you wanted to live somewhere secluded, and when I saw this, I used the money Mom gave me to buy it. We live here now. I know neither of us want kids, but if you ever do, there are spare rooms I can decorate. I'll even get a dog if you—

She grabs my hands to stop me, and I furrow my brows.

"Malachi," she says, her face going ghastly pale. "I don't want to live here."

I pull my hands free. *Do you want to live somewhere else? I can sell—it's fine. We can be together wherever you want.*

"No." She moves off me. "I mean... I don't want to live here... with you. Or anywhere with you. What's happened since the festival doesn't change the fact you nearly killed Dad. I don't forgive you for that."

My heart sinks. "Why?"

"Why?" she asks, a tear slipping down her cheek. "Are you really asking me that? Because I don't love you. I'm... We... No, Malachi."

"Y-You don't lo-love me?" I stutter the words, but I don't fucking care. She's a liar. She's lying, and I refuse to fucking take it.

I get off the bed and walk over to my combats, pulling my phone out. It takes me less than five seconds to find one of the voicemails she left me, and I play it while she sits up on the bed.

Sniffles, and then... "Malachi, where are you?" She sobs, as if she's hyperventilating. "I can't find you anywhere. Mom said you were released a few weeks ago—why haven't you come for me?"

She's crying, and I watch as her frown flattens, her shoulders hunching as she listens to herself, and she looks away as the voicemail keeps playing.

"I'm so, so sorry I didn't protect you. I should have told everyone what you meant to me, and I didn't. I was scared of the backlash, and everyone said you were vulnerable and that you were sick, that your obsession with me was down to you wanting to own something—someone. Me. And I was scared they were right."

She sniffs some more. "I want to know if anything was ever real for you. Any of it. If you tell me you love me, that I mean the world to you, then I'll admit that I feel the exact same. Because I do, Malachi. I love you so much it hurts."

I shut off the voicemail, and step forward, my body shaking with rage. "It was r-r-real. All o-of it was r-real. Everyth-thing was real. You mean th-the world t-t-to me. But you won't s-s-say it back, w-will you?"

She lowers her head and shakes it, and I feel like my entire world just collapsed.

Olivia's slipping through my fingers. What the fuck do I do?

"I am sorry," I say, fucking up the enunciation but who the fuck cares? "The spider. The knife. The cameras. All o-o-of it. I'm sorry." I close my eyes and blow out a breath. "I need you, Ol—" I stop, my heart racing so fast, I think it might stop.

"I don't need you," she murmurs, and I feel like I've been stabbed in the chest. "I'm getting married soon, Malachi—I signed an agreement. I can't back out. I won't. We have no chance in this life—don't you see?" She stands, and I gulp and step back as she wraps the duvet around her body. "Society would never accept us."

I grip the phone in my hand. "Fuck society." I don't think

my words have ever been clearer than right now. "Fuck everyone against us."

"You don't even know how to love properly. Your diagnosis proves that. Why would I give up a marriage for someone who can never feel the same way about me?"

I stay quiet, because she's right.

My version of love isn't enough for her—I love her, I do, but how am I supposed to know what's normal and what's not? My world revolves around her and always has. And if that's not a good-enough version of love for her, and I can't make her happy, then what's the point?

She goes through the dresser, shaking her head when she sees it's filled with clothes I bought for her over the last few months. She puts on underwear, slides yoga pants on, then grabs some other items.

She pulls on a shirt, buttons it up to her neck to hide the marks I gave her, then sits on the edge of the bed as she fixes her hair over her shoulder and puts on some socks.

I stay against the wall, my hands behind me, and try to think of everything possible to make her stay. Willingly. I want Olivia to choose me.

Please choose me.

Nobody ever chooses me.

She stands, slips on her shoes, and wipes under her eyes. "I won't tell anyone I saw you," she says, her head down. "Mom will want to know where I've been the last few days, so I'll need to lie and make up a story. If you let me leave, I'll forget this ever happened. Don't be difficult about this, Malachi. I'm leaving one way or another."

I can't answer. I just look at the ground as she moves towards me then stops. "Goodbye, Malachi. Please take care of yourself. Please."

Something weird is happening to me. My chest is sore, and my eyes feel immense pressure, and they're... wet. I think I might be crying for the first time in my life.

She opens the door, but I rush in front of her, blocking her exit as I drop to my knees and grab her hands. "Olivia," I whisper clearly. "Please don't leave me. Please stay with me."

Her sadness is all over her face—she's looking at me like I'm the one breaking her heart, her eyes following a tear as it slides down my cheek.

"Please," I beg. "Accept *my* v-version of love. Pl-ease. I love you, Ol-l-l—"

Olivia doesn't tell me she loves me back, or that she'll stay. She just gives me a warm smile and pulls her hand away before squeezing past me.

I don't turn around to watch her walk out of my life for good.

EPILOGUE
OLIVIA
2 weeks later

I don't recognize the person looking back at me as I stare at my reflection.

My bloodshot eyes are sunken, the makeup doing nothing to make me look like less of a zombie. Getting zero sleep and crying all night will do that to a person, I guess.

Mom steps in front of me, her expressionless face like stone as she fixes the curls on each side of my face. Her hands are shaking—the only sign she's feeling anything at all as she prepares me for my future husband. After all, she's been planning this day since she adopted me—she just had to find someone rich enough; a member of the elite.

Lucky me.

The white dress is hanging from a large rack—a corset with two skirts; one for length and another—an overskirt—for volume, which will make it so puffy that I'm definitely going to struggle to walk.

The itchy silk PJs my sister made me wear say "Team Bride," and I can't wait to burn them. I've managed to hide the marks Malachi left on my body with concealer, but I can feel them everywhere. They're reminders of what I'm leaving behind, even though I want to run to him.

Please don't leave me. Please stay with me.

"I don't want to do this," I tell Mom quietly. "Don't make me marry Xander."

She grins at me, but it's fake. Her eyes shine like glass. "We already signed the agreement, sweetheart. Xander is a very wealthy man who'll look after you."

I fight against the twist in my gut. "Why do you think my hair is blonde now? He's a controlling ass. He thinks I need to lose weight and says I'm to stay silent unless spoken to. He's a sexist pig who needs his balls chopped off."

Her hands, which have been fixing my newly dyed hair, pause. I think she's about to scold me for my language but asks, "He said that?"

"Yes," I reply. "I have the text messages to prove it. He keeps sending me links to weight-loss tablets and even implied he'd pay for breast implants and a nose job."

Molly chimes in, "I'd take the bigger boobs."

"Shut up, you're fourteen."

Mom lowers her eyes. "There's no way for us to back out. I'm sorry."

"Tell them the agreement is void. I don't want to marry him. I'll run away or put a bullet in my head. Tell him I have an STD or that I'm pregnant with another man's child. Anything."

"That's dramatic, Olivia."

"Better than being in an abusive marriage. You're sending me away to get beat up for opening my mouth then trampled on when I don't open my legs for him."

"Xander is a nice boy," she says blandly.

"He isn't a boy—he's older than me. And he's an asshole."

My sister hums. "I don't like him either," she says, crossing her arms and popping out her hip. "I vote we ditch here and go for ice cream."

My hand raises. "I second that."

Mom rolls her eyes. "Stop it, both of you. We just need to get through this day." Her voice falters at the end. "I'm sorry. I really am. My hands are tied here."

"Can't Dad do something?"

She gives me a stern look. "You keep your father out of this. I mean it."

I flatten my lips. "As soon as I walk down the aisle, me and you are done, Mom. I'll never speak to you again."

"Oh, come on, Olivia. You're twenty-six years old—act like it."

I take a deep breath, wanting to hurt her, to hit deep where it will haunt her. She's selling me to a monster, so the least I can do is ruin her day. "I was with Malachi when you were trying to call me."

"What do you mean you were with him?"

"I mean, I was *with* with him." I need to at least keep it PG, since my teen sister is listening in and she isn't aware of the ins and outs of his imprisonment. Not fully. "And I don't regret one second of it."

Her eyes widen. "What?" she sputters, looking for her words. "He nearly killed your father. You're engaged. He's… he's your brother, Olivia!"

"I'm aware of our position and what he's done," I grit. "He lost control. I won't defend him for attacking Dad, but we aren't related by blood, so no laws have been broken. You can't stop me from loving him."

God, that felt so good to say. A weight instantly lifts from my chest, and warmth gathers around my heart.

"I'm in love with Malachi," I say more firmly, more to myself, and Molly squeals with a hand clapped over her mouth. My heart rate picks up. "I hope he's down there waiting for me, and I hope he stops this wedding. I hope he saves me from Xander, since you're not doing shit to protect me. You've sold me my entire life. You sold my *virginity*—how cold can you be?"

She grips her necklace. "I was doing what I thought was best for you and the family. I was protecting you."

"Bullshit. The only one who ever protected me was

Malachi."

There's a knock at the door, and all three of us turn to see Dad pushing it open then rolling his wheelchair in. He pauses when he sees me, something passing through his eyes that I can't quite put my finger on. Sadness?

"May I speak with Olivia? Privately?"

Mom and Molly leave, but not before the latter leans in and kisses my cheek. "I should be totally grossed out that you have a crush on our foster brother, but I'm not. I think he'll show up."

My face heats, and I smile at her. "I don't think I'll be that lucky."

She shrugs. "We'll see."

As she skips out, she ruffles our father's hair and dodges him slapping her hand away, both of them laughing.

The door closes, and I take a deep breath. "I don't want this."

"I can tell. It's written all over your face. Why don't you want to marry Xander?"

My shoulders slump. "He's horrible, Dad."

"The real reason," he counters.

I freeze, not blinking as my hands fist. "He really is horrible—I was just telling Mom how he's already speaking to me like crap."

"Has he hurt you?"

I shake my head. "I think he will though. He... he sent a

team to my apartment to dye my hair two days ago—he said I was too dull, and he made them completely change my wardrobe."

His nostrils flare. "Anything else?"

My bottom lip trembles. Admitting to him that his attacker is the one who owns my heart is the ultimate betrayal. But something tells me he already knows.

He clears his throat and rolls forward a little. "You can tell me."

"I love him," I say, the words broken in my throat as a tear slips down my cheek. "Malachi."

The fact his expression doesn't budge tells me a lot.

"I know it's wrong to you—I know that I shouldn't be in love with someone I call my brother, but I can't help it. I've loved him since forever. I… I can't remember a time I haven't been in love with him. Even when I testified, I regretted it instantly. I turned my back on him when he was vulnerable. I've been living in a nightmare ever since."

Nodding, he sighs. "He's sick, Olivia. He isn't capable of making you happy."

"But he does make me happy." I shake my head. "He nearly killed you, and I still can't fall out of love with him." My face crumples as I let it all out. "I'm such a horrible daughter."

"You're human," he says, softening his tone. "Come here, angel."

I move forward, crouching down so he can take my hand.

"I'm going to get you out of this. Not necessarily so you can run into your bro— Malachi's arms, but I want you to be free from this life. Your mother—she's insistent on power and traditions. She signed the agreement without my knowledge."

"What happens if I don't marry Xander?"

"I really don't know. We can figure this all out after the ceremony. His family is quite dangerous. I don't want you getting hurt if a war breaks out."

"He's going to hurt me regardless. After the ceremony, h-he'll…"

He'll drag me to the honeymoon suite and violently fuck me. No thanks. I'll happily throw myself from the roof before he can get anywhere near me. Death is a better option.

I take a deep breath, not seeing any other way around this unless it's me in a body bag. "I'll go, but please help me divorce him. And promise me you won't let Mom control Molly the way she controlled me growing up." My voice drops firmer. "Promise me."

"I promise," he replies, smiling faintly. "I promise to do everything in my power to protect you and your sister."

After a minute of me crying, he wipes under my eyes with a napkin.

"Are you mad at me?" I ask. "Because of how I feel about Malachi?"

"I could never be mad at you. Am I dumbfounded by your decision on who you want to be with? Certainly. You really do see the good in him."

I nod.

"I can try to forgive him. From what I know from the PIs I have following him, he started therapy two weeks ago."

Wait, Dad had private investigators following Malachi? Does he already know I was with him then? Perhaps Malachi dodged them, or whoever he hired is terrible at their job because he technically kidnapped me.

"So you already knew I was…?"

"I didn't tell your mother, and I knew he wouldn't hurt you. I pulled my PI away soon after he spoke to you on his motorbike."

Despite the internal panic, my chest tightens. "You said he started therapy?"

"Yes, angel. He sees a speech-language pathologist now too. He enquired the day you returned home, and I made sure he was seen the following day. That tells me he's trying to be better. We wanted this for him for years. He's even been prescribed medication."

"He never wanted to be medicated. He liked being in control."

"He was never in control," Dad replies. "He was just really good at hiding it."

Someone knocks on the door, informing us that the groom is impatiently waiting for his bride.

I stand, and Dad looks up at me. "I want to try to make amends, but it won't be instant. He turned my life upside down." He gestures to his chair. "I don't think I can forgive him easily."

"If he's trying… could you try too?" I wipe under my eyes and breathe. "For me—please?"

I know it's selfish to ask, but what else do I do? I'm about to be dragged away from this life—as Xander oh so nicely put it when he stood at my door last night and told me we're moving to Canada for his new business deal next week. If Malachi at least has Dad on his side, maybe he'll be okay. Maybe, with support around him, he'll adjust.

Dad nods then tells me to take a few minutes to calm down and meet at the entrance of the hall where the ceremony is being held. The door closes with a click, and I glance around the empty room.

My future is waiting for me—a cruel, horrid fate. Why didn't I stay with him in that farmhouse in the woods? Why didn't I kiss him and admit that I'm madly in love with him?

"Are you watching me?" I ask out loud.

Silence.

I turn on the spot, searching for a camera. "Are you planning on stopping the wedding?"

Please. Please, please, please, Malachi. I'm sorry.

230

Tears slide down my cheeks. There aren't any shadows hiding in the corner either. "I should have chosen you."

Of every mistake I've made in my life, not choosing Malachi has been my worst. He begged me on his knees with tears in his eyes, something I never thought I'd witness, and I walked away from him. I didn't fight. I didn't even *try* to make it work between us.

Malachi, despite all his craziness, deserves better than me.

Mom won.

She groomed me for this day—and being the obedient daughter, I'm too scared to disappoint her, to ruin her plans after she saved me from my old life.

That's all I can think about as I pull on my dress and stare at myself in the floor-to-ceiling mirror. I should be crying with happiness, excited yet nervous, impatiently waiting to spend the rest of my life with the man I love.

But I'm not.

Ten minutes later, the train of my wedding dress drags down the grand staircase as my dad waits at the bottom, clutching his walking stick as he rises from his wheelchair. It'll keep him on his feet until he's done walking me up the aisle. He smiles when he sees me in my dress, the one Mom made me wear even though I said I hated it.

Everyone is waiting for me—my future husband, who's probably forgotten my name, and my future family, who care more about status than anything else.

Molly is one of my bridesmaids. She joined the family not long after Malachi was sent to prison. At first, the courts were unsure whether to place her in my family's care, but she's had a blast with us.

She wishes she'd met Malachi. She's aware he's a little insane and violent, that he beat up Dad. But she thinks he blacked out—that it wasn't deliberate. She said he looked like he'd be a fun big brother from the pictures I showed her, and I admit, he really was a fun brother growing up. We did everything together. Set aside all the things we shouldn't have been doing, he was also my best friend.

Those eight years without him were torture, but the last two weeks? Hell.

He broke into my apartment the day after I walked away from him and took all the cameras out. He left a note telling me he'd drawn a mustache on Mom's face months ago and I should wipe it, and that all my wine bottles are spiked.

He turned his phone off—disconnected it.

As much as I can't be with him, I think I would've loved it if he was watching me. But I know he isn't anymore. He's just... gone. There hasn't even been any communication between us.

I made the wrong decision.

Now I can't do anything but hook my arm through my dad's and walk.

"You look beautiful," Dad says. "I promise to get you out of this arrangement. Just smile and stay calm."

I try to smile and fail.

I don't look up as we approach the double doors. There's music playing on the other side. I halt, taking a deep breath as "Here Comes the Bride" starts, and the doors open to reveal everyone seated in their chairs. I scan them, looking for black hair, a smirk, a cheeky grin or a wink, but he isn't here—I wish he was though.

"Breathe, angel."

I make it halfway down the aisle before my lungs give up, and the panic sets in. I stop abruptly, my dad nearly tripping over his walking stick, and I look up at him. "I... I can't do this."

"Olivia," a stern voice comes, and I look up to find Xander glaring at me. "Walk towards me now."

I turn to Dad. "Please let me go."

He looks lost, glancing between me and Mom. Xander's family members are glaring at me like I'm a spoiled brat. Abigail, Molly, and Anna are standing beside Xander in their bridesmaid dresses, none of them looking shocked—more pleased than anything.

Xander shakes his head. "Keep fucking walking, Olivia. Don't embarrass me."

Molly scowls at him.

Mom steps away from her seat, and for the first time in

forever, she doesn't force me to keep going. She sighs and nods at me.

"Go," Dad says, kissing my cheek. "We'll deal with them. Be happy, angel."

I drop the overpriced flowers I'm carrying and grab the front of my dress, turning and running out of there. I leave my heels where they slip off and yank my veil off as I rush out the front entranceway.

I spin and look around for him, but I can't see him.

"Malachi!" I yell, unclipping the band around my waist to rid myself of the overskirt, leaving it where it falls as I run towards the gates, pushing out of them and gasping for air as I flag down a cab and give them directions to the place he took me at Halloween.

His house. Ours. Something I walked away from.

My body shakes uncontrollably as I watch the town disappear and be replaced by trees. How far away is it? Ten minutes go by. Twenty. Fifty. An hour.

I only know the address because I had to call a cab when I left him and the driver was able to locate me.

I climb out of the car as soon as I reach my destination and stop when I see Malachi standing by the metal gate, disbelief written all over his face as he pushes it open and takes a step towards me.

He's topless, face and chest glistening post-workout, black

hair wild and curly, with a pair of sweats sitting low on his hips.

Malachi has been the one for me since forever.

He's my forever. My heaven and hell.

"Olivia?"

So clear. So clear and pure and full of love.

I laugh out a cry and run at him, launching myself into his strong arms that instantly wrap around me. His eyes are wide, searching my face and lifting to my blonde hair.

"Wh—"

"You're mine, Malachi. You're mine and I'm yours and I love you more than words can explain. Please forgive me. Please. I want you. I want to be with you, build a life with you, and make memories with you. I want to wake up every morning with you by my side. I want you to chase me through these woods and take me against a tree. I want everything you have to give. All of it. Everything. Because I choose you. I—"

Malachi kisses me into silence.

It's a claiming kiss that takes my breath away.

He grins against my lips. "I love you, Olivia."

I giggle and wrap my legs around his waist, my face sore from how hard I'm smiling. "I love you too. Will you take me inside our home and show me how much you love me?"

He shakes his head and drops me to my feet. "I want to rip that fucking dress from your body then make you bleed all over it."

Butterflies are going wild inside me, my chest rising and falling with anticipation. "I dare you," I tease. "I dare you to chase me and make me beg for it."

Malachi groans and snatches my jaw, pressing a harsh kiss to my mouth before shoving me back, grinning and gesturing to the woods.

"Run, little stranger."

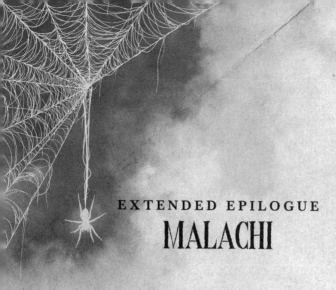

EXTENDED EPILOGUE
MALACHI

She vanishes into the forest, that fucking dress clinging to her skin. The dress that'll be ripped from her body as soon as I catch her.

I'll let her run, get worked up, and put some fear and paranoia into her before I claim what's rightfully mine.

I inhale, my nostrils flaring as I tamp down my rage at the thought of her marrying someone else. I was giving her space to think about her choice while still watching from afar. I'd planned to hang the bastard with his own tie on their wedding night. Or kick the door of their honeymoon suite off its hinges and blow his fucking head off for even thinking he could have Olivia.

She's mine. She's been mine since the moment we met.

And she'll remain my goddamn property.

I'll be the one who keeps her safe, holds her hand when she's scared, fucks her when she needs my cock. I'll kiss her and remind her that I'm not her real brother; I'm not a sibling with any blood relation.

I've accepted I'm sick, because I fucking love when she calls me her brother while she's taking my cock like the best little sister there is.

The world can fuck off, and our family can just deal with us being together.

I walk back into the house. In just fourteen days, I've got it almost fully renovated. Sleeping has been a struggle, so I needed the distraction, something to keep my hands busy while I watched the monitors lining one of my walls.

I pull open the toolbox and smirk when I see the screwdriver. I study the bulb handle, flip it in my hand twice, then slam the box shut.

Above the fireplace, a picture of us is cradled in a frame I made from one of the trees I cut down. She's smiling at me while I'm trying to push her face away. I remember she'd just whispered something filthy in my ear—probably something to do with our lessons.

The lessons.

Is it possible for me to talk her into teaching me like before? I'll happily act the innocent brother while she forces me to my knees and tells me how to eat her pussy again.

I was never clueless—inexperienced, yes—but never clueless. I'd watched porn with my cock in my hand and felt unsatisfied, yet I'd watched and watched. I'd stayed hidden within her bedroom while she made herself come, learning from the shadows what she likes.

Being a virgin at nineteen didn't bother me. There was something more important than fucking anyone who threw themselves at me.

Olivia was more important. I knew to wait. I knew that one day, even if we were in our fucking thirties, I'd bury my cock in my sister and make her moan my name so damn loud. I'd have the sound in my ears until the day I died.

I've never been afraid of dying—it's inevitable. But the thought of dying and leaving Olivia behind? Of leaving her with all the poisonous toxicity in the world? That terrifies me. She can't trust anyone, especially not Mom.

But she can trust me. She can always trust me.

I push open the back door and glance out into the forest. It's been ten, maybe fifteen minutes. She'll be panicking now that the sun is starting to set and night is nearing. Pretty soon, she won't be able to see much.

Why does that make me uneasy?

I grip the screwdriver and crack my neck from side to side, still feeling the touch of her kiss on my lips.

I need more.

My eyes flicker around my surroundings as I walk slowly out of the backyard. I still need to fix it up. There's a half-built motorbike—a project my therapist thinks will help me focus—

and supplies I ended up not using while doing the house.

I push open the small, creaky metal gate and pause, listening, but all I can hear are the rustling leaves as the wind picks up and the drizzle of rain starting to hit the canopy of the trees.

A storm is coming.

"Tell me, Olivia," I say. My words are still a little messy but clearer, since all I've been doing is talking to myself and a speech therapist for the last two weeks. "When you got into that dress, did you imagine him peeling it off? Did you put on a lace garter for him to take off with his teeth?"

I'm annoying myself with my words. I'm getting angry.

But I can't stop.

"Did he touch you?"

My voice is low, a threat, and I think my heart might beat out of my chest at the thought of anyone putting their hands on her. I've already dealt with the others who dared to go near her when I was locked up. Thankfully, and luckily, I made sure I'd never get caught and sent back to prison.

"He'd never make you feel the way I do."

No one could ever make her feel the way I do. Ever. And if they do, I'll kill them.

I hear a branch snapping in the distance, and instead of running straight for her, I taunt her some more. "You cried for me." My steps are slow, calculated, my fingers wrapping tightly around the screwdriver handle as I edge closer to where she is.

"I watched you," I say louder, my eyes on the darkness ahead of me, knowing she's hiding behind a large tree trunk. "You had no idea I was right there. Waiting. Always fucking waiting for you, Olivia."

The rain gets heavier, soaking me, drops falling from the strands of hair hanging over my forehead. "It's your turn to wait, little sister. I hope it kills you. I hope you're shaking in your wedding dress, wondering when I'll grab you from the shadows and fuck you against a tree."

My cock strains against my shorts, fucking aching to get inside her.

"I'll take your beautiful mouth first," I say. "Then I'll bury myself deep in your ass."

There's a whimper, and I smirk. "I like it when you're scared—fighting me like you could actually win. You never had a chance of beating me, Olivia."

I up my pace as I hear more branches snapping.

She's running.

I flip the screwdriver in my palm. As soon as I see the flash of white from her wedding dress, I start chasing her. I grit my teeth and dodge branches, ducking as she stops and tries to throw one at me, missing me by an inch. She screams and turns to run again.

I spot the smile on her face.

My darling sister is nearly as sadistic as me. She likes to be hunted and caught and fucked. She once told me she wanted to be chased through a graveyard, but unfortunately, this forest will have to do. I'll chase her in here every day for the rest of our lives.

The forest edge comes into sight. There's a small drop to a river ahead. Will she jump?

My heart ricochets in my chest as I stop fucking around and properly chase her. I catch up to her in no time, grabbing a fistful of her hair and dragging her off her feet. She screams and rips her nails into the skin of my wrist, kicking her heels into my shins.

I push her chest against the closest tree and hold her there with one hand while I put the screwdriver between my teeth, yanking at the back of her dress hard enough to rip it.

She whimpers, her hands still slapping at my wrists to get herself free. I love the fight.

I pull at the dress again, splitting the material to the small of her back, then reach forward and pinch her hard, pebbled nipple and twist.

Her knees buckle, but my hold on her hair keeps her upright.

"I found you," I whisper against her ear. "I'm never letting you go now." I tear more at her dress, making the material fall down her legs and pool at her feet. "You're mine."

"And you're mine," she breathes, pushing her ass against me.

I grin and turn her around, grabbing her jaw. "Yours. You promise you won't run away again? I'll chase you."

Olivia takes my thumb into her mouth and sucks on it. I press down on her tongue and push until I feel her throat contract. "Such a good little sister."

My dick is begging me to fuck her, to free it from my pants and shove into her, but I keep my thumb in her mouth and use my hold to bring her to her knees.

"Take my cock out," I demand, pulling my thumb from her mouth and dragging her bottom lip down. "I want these lips around it."

The rain trickles through the canopy, droplets falling on her face as she looks up at me while reaching for my waistband. She curls her fingers into the material and pulls, my cock springing free.

Her eyes flicker back up to me as she wraps her fingers around my thickness, and I glare at the engagement ring on her finger.

I snatch her wrist and pull the piece of junk off, scowling at it. "The only time you ever wear a ring like this is when I put one there, do you understand?"

She nods. "Yes."

I fist it in my palm and launch it through the forest, not giving a fuck where it goes, then grab a handful of her hair and force my cock into her mouth. She gags around it, taking half before she wraps her fingers around me again, swallowing around my swollen crown.

My eyes roll as she sucks, bobbing her head as I let go of her and press both my hands to the tree behind her. "Fuck, your mouth feels so good, Olivia."

The praise makes her go faster, sucking harder, using her tongue to massage around the tip and taking more of me. I hit the back of her throat and take over, holding the back of her head as I thrust in and out.

She gasps as I pull free. "I'm coming inside you," I tell her, pushing her to lie down on her dress. "Part your legs. Let me see what I own."

Her legs open, showing me her pretty little pussy, which is covered with a scrap of soaked fabric. Her eyes widen as I pick up the screwdriver I dropped as I lower to my knees between her legs.

"Wait..." She hesitates, leaning up on her elbows.

"Hmm?" I grasp at her inner thigh and move the handle over the material, rubbing upwards to her clit. "You want me to stop?"

Her lips part, and then there's a slight shake of her head. My girl is so damn brave.

When I lean down and drag my tongue against her pussy, she moans and drops fully onto her back again. I suck on her clit through her underwear, biting and ripping the fabric to make a hole.

I close my eyes and savor the taste of her.

All mine.

She cries out as I force my tongue inside her, then I pull my face away and push the handle of the screwdriver in as far as it can go, chewing my bottom lip and watching her pussy swallow the handle—Olivia's soaked, throbbing, needy little pussy.

She tries to crush her legs together when I press my mouth to her clit again, moaning, fisting her fingers into my hair and tugging.

She's so perfect. I'm starting to think this is all a dream. Maybe I'm still in prison and imagining all this? That's fine—as long as I never wake up, I'm good to stay in this bubble with her.

She screams, her back arching, as I start thrusting the screwdriver. Knowing her orgasm is coming, I trap her clit between my teeth and pull the screwdriver out, dropping it so I can push two fingers inside her. Her inner walls clutch me as I curl them then fuck her hard and fast with them while I feast on her clit.

Her orgasm hits, and her screams echo through the woods.

The sound is enough to drive me insane. I pull away completely, shove down my shorts and briefs, and position myself between her legs. I grab her face. "You left me for eight years, and then you left me again. There won't be a third time, Olivia."

"Never," she says desperately, rolling her hips so the tip of my cock is pushing through her entrance and making her whimper. "Please, Malachi."

"Are you sorry?"

She nods. "I am. I'm so, so, so sorry. I love you. I've always loved you."

My nose grazes hers as I lower my face, kissing her softly. I take her bottom lip between mine, sucking lightly, then I do the same with the top. "Will you marry me?"

"Yes," she moans as I push into her, feeling her walls strangling my cock, her orgasm still lingering. "Yes. A million times yes. We'll find a way."

Fuck. This is really happening. Olivia is mine.

Her eyes roll as I rock into her, the dress getting dirty and soaked from both the rain and Olivia's pussy. I go deeper, kissing her harder, needing to stay in this moment forever.

Her legs wrap around me as I thrust, my spine already tingling with the tightening heat building in my balls. She moves with me, meeting each thrust, kissing me, loving me the way I always wanted to be loved.

Our foreheads touch and our bare chests rub together, her breasts and hard nipples trapped between us.

"I love you," she whispers in my ear, taking my lobe between her teeth. "I love you, I love you, I love you. I'm so sorry I wasn't strong enough, but I am now. Please forgive me."

My balls tighten, my muscles tensing everywhere as she starts moaning louder, another orgasm washing over her as her eyes glaze over and her grip on my body turns painful. Her nails sink into my skin as she cries, whimpers, fucking begs me to stay with her.

Not that I'd ever leave her.

After I fill her with every drop of my cum, I stay inside her for far too long. She's shaking, trembling from coming so hard. I keep my head on her shoulder, and her hand strokes up and down my back as she tells me over and over that I'm hers.

I straighten my arms, sliding out of her. She grins up at me, tears in her eyes. "You might need to carry me home."

I laugh, kissing her. She giggles as I stand and pull her up into my arms, holding her to my chest as we leave the dress, screwdriver, and my sweats in the forest while I carry her to the house.

She doesn't take her eyes off me.

When we get inside, I run us a bath. We lie in it until the water goes cold, reminiscing about the times we shared growing up. After we eat, I take her to bed and make love to her.

I've never made love before. I had no idea what it felt like.

I've fucked Olivia. I've claimed her, ruined her in ways a brother shouldn't, but I've never made love to her.

It's… different. Slow. Sensual.

I didn't know I could love her more, but I do. Everything is heightened as I take her in our bed. She flips us so she's on top, and even the way she's riding me is slow, emotional, and I can't take my fucking eyes off her.

After we both finish, we lie in each other's arms. There's no other shoe dropping; there's no pause while we wait for something bad to happen.

Is this what it's like to be happy? I like it. Surely our parents will understand?

"I'm worried about what Xander will do."

I narrow my eyes. "He won't get near you. I'll deal with him."

"You're starting to get your life back, Malachi. You were in prison for nearly a decade. Please don't get involved in this. I shouldn't have brought it up. Xander isn't in my life, and he never will be. Just... be with me and forget the world. Please?"

A muscle in my jaw ticks. "You can't ask me to do that, Olivia. From the moment I met you, I swore to myself I'd protect you. I've done a fucking shitty job of that so far, so I'm not going to sit around knowing he's out there and a threat."

She's scared of him. I should do something about that. I couldn't protect my mother from all the drug dealers and addicts who were constantly in and out of my house. All I could do was hide under my bed with my pet spider, who never wanted to talk back to me.

Every day and night, we would hide under my bed. He was

my best friend. But he never ever spoke, so why would I? He was happy without using his voice. I could be happy as well. He was my comforter. My protector. If he could conceal his voice and be brave enough to hide under my bed and not cry, then I could too.

It was the start of the new me. They wanted to hear me scream while they pushed the needle into my arm, so I didn't. I was starved, thin, weak, but at least I had power over my speech. They wouldn't take that from me too, because I hid it somewhere only Olivia could find it.

They wanted to hear me beg them to save my mom, and I couldn't.

Just like what happened with Spikey eight years ago, they killed my spider. They thought it was funny to make me watch while my bio-mom was dying on the floor. I couldn't save her, but I can save Olivia.

She grabs my face. "No, Malachi."

Yes, Malachi. It's fine. She doesn't need to know when I remove him from the equation. She'll see the reports that he's missing, and by then, the issue will be solved. She can yell at me while I fuck her.

"Promise me you won't do anything that will get you into trouble? Dad can fix it all."

"Hmm," I say. "Tell me what you want in life." I change the subject and lower my head, kissing the tip of her nose. "Tell me, so I can give it to you."

"I just want you."

I smirk down at her. "That's all?"

"My whole life, Mom has pushed marriage on me to the point that it holds no meaning to me unless I'm marrying you. And kids? I've never imagined myself as a mother—I think I'd be terrible at it. But…" She raises her shoulder shyly. "Maybe one day."

My smile drops. I'd give her anything she wanted. But a kid? "What if they're just like me?"

Her brow furrows. "There's nothing wrong with you."

"You really think that?" Even I know there's a lot wrong with me. That's why I decided to go to therapy—the meds are a little intense, but I can manage them. I'd do anything to be normal enough for Olivia. "My therapist said I have a lot to work on, but I'll change. I promise."

She grins, wrapping her arms around my neck and bringing my face to hers to whisper, "I love everything about you. I never want you to change."

I kiss her—the only girl I've ever imagined giving my heart to. It might be a little black, a little jagged around the edges, and my mind might be a little wild, but she owns them.

Olivia owns my mind, body, and soul. She did when we were kids, when we were teens, when we were giving in and letting go. Even when I had her chained up in the basement, she had a hold over me.

I had it in my head that I wanted revenge on her—I now know I just wanted her back.

And guess fucking what?

I got her back. She chose me.

Olivia actually chose me, and I intend to keep her.

THE END... or is it?

ABOUT THE AUTHOR

Leigh Rivers is a Scottish Biomedical Scientist who has ventured into the world of writing dark, morally gray characters with rollercoaster storylines to drive her readers wild.

When she isn't reading, writing on her laptop, or gaming until ridiculous hours, she dances at the pole studio, goes to the gym, and walks her four dogs with her two sons and husband.

You can find Leigh on her socials:
Instagram - @authorleighrivers
Facebook - @authorleighrivers
TikTok - @authorleighrivers